G R JORDAN

The Horror Weekend

A Highlands and Islands Detective Thriller

"There are hunters, and there are victims. By your discipline, cunning, obedience, and alertness, you will decide if you are a hunter or a victim."

Jim Mattis, former US Secretary of Defense

Contents

Foreword

This story is set in the idyllic yet sometimes harsh landscape of the Isle of Harris, located in the north-western part of Scotland. Although set amongst known towns and lochs, note that all persons and specific places are fictional and not to be confused with actual buildings and structures that exist and which have been used as an inspirational canvas on which to tell a completely fictional story.

Prologue

Macleod sat restless in the chair, his dressing gown wrapped up tight around him. Watching Hope in the bed, he imagined the warmth within those sheets and the sheer comfort of being there. It had been an hour ago that she had pushed back the cover in her sleep and exposed her shoulders and the flimsy top she was wearing in bed. Her red hair was splayed across pillows and she looked like the essence of sleep.

He stared at the clock on the wall trying to stop his imagination from dwelling any further on the woman sleeping in his bed. Jane could never know. How would he explain it? Sometimes things are just forced on you. No, they would never speak of it.

Why did they make these large houses with wooden floors, thought Macleod; *it's so cold.* The floor had an occasional worn rug covering it but was generally exposed. The room was such a weird mix—a modern television on the wall and then a somewhat ancient cupboard on the far wall. The furniture, a wardrobe that belonged with Queen Victoria and a bedside table that could have come from a Swedish furniture superstore.

This party was like that too, such a mix of people, and with so little in common apart from one or two of them being idiots. *Yes, idiots,* he thought, *I'm not being harsh. But then I never did understand the world of glamour and personality.* Why on earth had the boss managed to get herself an invitation to this, even if her husband was a friend of David Macaulay, the host? And then there was all the roleplaying, making people dress up. He didn't appreciate being lumbered with the investigator role in some shoddy reproduction of a horror plot. Fake graphics, fake ghosts, and fake sounds. Just all so fake when behind it, maybe there was something more sinister going on. It could not have been an accident. He couldn't put his finger on why but his gut was screaming at him.

Hope clearly didn't believe it. She was more at home amongst the nonsense and even flirted somewhat with the giant of a man who looked like he was from a magazine cover. Macleod was used to seeing her dressed for work and found some of her garb to be too revealing for his conservative upbringing. He hadn't known where to look. Or rather he had and was trying to stop himself. And not just Hope, there was that Welsh girl. She was happy for people to look. Although there was something else about her, too inquisitive, more than just interest. *She could almost be one of us*, he thought.

He heard footsteps from the hall outside. When they had retired into the room a few hours ago, he had locked the door, making sure it had closed correctly. Hope had looked at him as if he was mad but he hadn't made it to this stage as a detective without trusting his instinct. His partner—that is, his work partner—asleep in his bed and without him, was a good detective. She was conscientious, could even read a lot of people, and often had angles and takes he didn't, being from a different time. But her gut instinct was not as honed as his.

2

One of the perks of being an old fart!

The landing outside led to a balcony which he had seen earlier in the day. A drop of a few floors to the front entrance was kept safe by a railing that reached Macleod's hips. It had only been a brief look as they had made their way down after dressing in these ridiculous costumes. Now in the early hours of the morning, there was a storm at full tilt and he could hear it in the background of the night. But the step on the wooden floorboards of the landing cut through the background weather.

A sudden chill came across the floor and blew up his trousers, tingling the hairs on his shin. Whoever it was must have opened the door to the balcony. *Who in their right mind would take a walk outside tonight?* And then that gut instinct came again.

"Hey, when you said you'd take the chair I thought you were at least going to sleep." Hope had sat up in bed and when Macleod looked over, he found himself staring at her tight fitting pyjama top, hugging her body. Without hesitation, he grabbed his large woollen pullover from a chair and threw it at her.

"Put that on; it's cold."

Hope grabbed the top and hauled it on. "Sorry. I should have kept the covers up. But it was you who invited me to bed."

Macleod's eyes narrowed and he turned away, walking slowly towards the door. Hope occupied a funny space in his mind and heart. He liked her, respected her. He even saw her as a trusted police partner, even a friend, but he struggled not to enjoy how she looked. It cut against his Presbyterian upbringing and he did not know if it would ever leave. He tried to listen to what was happening outside and ignore Hope climbing out of the bed.

"What's up?"

"Someone moving," said Macleod. "Opened the door to the balcony."

"Is that what that bloody draft is? Some people don't give a shit about others."

Macleod raised two metaphorical eyebrows. Her language was so coarse, not befitting a woman. And then he heard a scream.

As quickly as he could, he unlocked the door and scanned the dark hallway. There was no one about the ornate landing but the door was still open to the balcony and the wind blew hard down the opening between bedrooms and sent a shiver through Macleod. Despite his costume, he was still feeling the cold from outside.

Macleod ran to the balcony, fighting through the wind and reached the open stonework and railing. There was no one there but he saw the footprints in the fresh snow. There was commotion from inside and he heard someone ask what was happening. Instinctively, he looked over the railings. Below, he saw the pointed railings that ended in spiked tops, hemming in small borders of flowers before the house. Snow covered the flower beds and, in the dark, provided a greyness to the general black of the night. But he saw the darker patches. And then he saw the figure hunched over the spikes, two of which had penetrated and come through the body.

Hope was on his shoulder looking down. "Bloody hell, Seoras. Poor bastard. Jump?"

"I doubt it," said Macleod, his eyes straining in the dark to see an object. "Rarely do people stab themselves in the back before jumping."

Chapter 01

"Y ou want me to go to Harris in this weather? You know the storm that's coming in?"

Macleod paced the kitchen as he heard the request from his boss. He was due back at work tomorrow after his two weeks off and was not looking forward to trying to get about the office in the melee that was due from the north. Ripping winds, possibly over one hundred miles per hour, localized gusts, and a snowfall that was set to make every kid's day. Schools might close, lots of traffic problems, and a lot of paperwork to go back to.

As his boss detailed her request, he watched Jane enter the kitchen, wrapped in her dressing gown, following her shower. She had practically moved in and never seemed to be away from the place, which did not bother Macleod at all. He traced her bare legs up to where the gown hung over her posterior and smiled. He had been brought up on a strict policy of no sex before marriage but here in his later years he had decided there was no time to hang about. And it was not as if he was putting it about, a term his mother had coined for *those type of men*.

Jane mouthed at him if he wanted coffee and he nodded. Usually he made his own but Jane got the privilege of being allowed to go near his treasured real beans and grinder. Yes, she made a cup that was too strong, filling the filter up to high heaven with coffee. But she usually brought him a morning cup to his bed and the view that accompanied it was better than any coffee. Well . . . yes it was.

"So will you go, Seoras?" The voice on the line had used his real name. Not Macleod, not Inspector, just Seoras. His boss had also got him tickets to the opera recently, front row seats. He had hated it but Jane had loved the whole night and Macleod's stock had gone up even higher than the stratospheric heights he was already at. He was not getting away from this request.

"Jane," he said and watched the love in his life turn around. "I need to go north for a few days. Should only be two days, three at most."

Jane nodded and turned back to the coffee production. Then she spun back. "You were going to be working anyway, so fine. I'll go stay with my sister for a few days, she could probably do with help, what with the storm coming."

Jane's sister had lost the use of her legs in a car accident and whilst generally self-sufficient, was looked after by her older sister on occasion. Macleod had seen Anna several times and she had been engaging like Jane. There were only the two sisters in the family now, no children. Unlike Jane, Anna was not into her forties and was only past thirty, being a very late decision by her parents, as she put it. Having spent only a few punctuated days with her, Macleod wondered how she did not have single men falling at her feet. Maybe it was the chair. It was not PC to mention that these days but bias was still prevalent even if not talked about.

"So where are you going again?" asked Jane.

6

"Isle of Harris."

"Is that the Hebrides?"

"Yes," said Macleod, "one down from Lewis. We really need to take you up there, show you my roots. Let you see my past, see where . . ." He nearly blurted it out. Nearly started talking about his deceased wife, Hope, again.

"Where you met Hope," said Jane. "Where you guys got together, where you first stayed out all night, where you first did it outside!"

Macleod laughed. "You are outrageous."

"And you need to understand, I am not jealous of Hope. She was a big part of your life, she was so special to you. She helped mould this man before me that I want, that I can't help but love despite his blurting insecurity about his previous love. You can talk to me about her."

"I know."

"Do you?" asked Jane. "I know more about you than you think, Seoras Macleod. I can tell things about you that you don't even know yourself."

"I thought I was the detective."

"For instance," said Jane, refusing to be side tracked, "I know for a fact that you would rather make the coffee yourself. I know I am in a special place being allowed to even touch these beans." She giggled at his horrified face. "But most of all, I know that what really lets you give up your precious coffee to the hands of a philistine like me is the fact that I'm making it in just a dressing gown and you are hoping to enjoy the sight while I work away at the coffee."

Macleod's face fell. "That's a bit harsh. Maybe I'm just sharing, offering a piece of me to you."

Jane laughed and turned back to the coffee machine. She

lifted her dressing gown so her bare buttocks were in full view. "That's where your eyes are at." Laughing, she turned back around and walked up to Macleod wrapping her arms around him, kissing him on the cheek. "Don't ever take your eyes off me. Call me an insecure daft mare but you damn well stare, Seoras Macleod." He gripped her tightly. "And let me know about Hope Macleod. She sounds like she was my kind of girl." He gripped Jane even tighter.

The wind rattled around the kitchen window and Macleod looked out of it whilst holding the embrace. Snow was falling, flitting into the glow of the streetlight, a dancing swirl of God's sheer mercy. *Dear God, what have you given me in these arms? Thank you.*

Breaking off the embrace, Jane grabbed the coffee from the kitchen work top. "You're only getting three days, Macleod, mind. Not a day longer. You hear me." Macleod nodded, his face lit up by this light in his life. "Good, now get up those stairs; you can pack in the morning. Once you've reminded me how young we are again, you can tell me all about the trip."

It was dark when Macleod arose, showered, and dressed for his trip. Since he had been dragged upstairs the night before, he had to try to pack in the blackness of early morning until Jane complained he was making too much noise and switched the lights on. When he stumbled down the stairs, she was standing in a pair of jogging bottoms and a large jumper, her hair dishevelled and eyes bleary. But this was her home now, he thought. He was feeling more confident in their relationship and the future looked bright.

As he stared out of the window, Jane wrapped her arms around him and placed her head on his back. His enjoyment of the moment was broken up by the arrival of a car. A horn blurted into the morning silence.

It's five in the morning, Hope, a little decorum, he thought. Jane kissed him goodbye, told him to take care, and then stood at the door as he walked to his awaiting partner.

"Morning, Seoras. Why am I up at this God forsaken hour to go to a party?" asked a yawning Hope.

"You have the privilege of a couple of nights away; there's plenty at the station who would jump at it."

"Let them fling themselves this way—I want my bed."

Macleod laughed and waved goodbye to Jane as Hope drove the car slowly down the Glasgow street. The air was cold outside and the wind was picking up again. There had already been a snowfall and the city was draped in a blanket that covered the grey grime but which turned to a wet slush at the roadside.

"Have you been back to Lewis at all since our first case?" asked Hope as they drove.

"No. I'm going to take Jane up, let her see where I'm from. Let her see where my Hope died. I think it might help me." Macleod shifted uncomfortably after saying this. Despite having Jane in his life and thoroughly enjoying her company and love, he still had a pain inside that did not want to leave.

"That's good. You two seem to be getting on well. She's really lovely, Seoras. You fell on your feet there."

"And what about you? I really struggle to believe you're single, Hope. I mean . . ." Macleod stopped. He had almost blurted out how great she looked but in a much more vulgar way. These days it was harder to compliment a woman. It was offensive to comment about how good a woman looked. He loved that Jane didn't care about how he looked at her but Hope was not his lover and he should be more guarded with

9

his comments. After all, it was too easy with a woman such as Hope for the mind to get carried away, especially when working so closely.

"Mean what?" asked Hope.

"Your personality. It's very contagious." Macleod smiled inwardly.

"Very good effort. We'll make a modern man of you yet," laughed Hope.

Glasgow airport was its usual mass of people in the early morning and Macleod resented the rush and panic to get through security and then have to sit down for a half hour waiting for the aircraft. Rather than wait in the small area given over to the passengers for the Islands, Macleod dragged Hope to a cafe area and ordered two bacon rolls and coffee. Through the large windows, he could see snow ploughs moving along the runway and it made him shiver. Ten years ago, the cold did not bother him but these days he was feeling the chill more than ever. Beside him, Hope sat in a long black coat, laid open with a white blouse underneath. She looked warm. *Lucky her!*

After an hour's delay, they were hurtling down the runway on the small thirty-odd seat plane, the noise of whose engines made chatting on the flight almost impossible. Macleod grimaced as spots of turbulence caused him to think he was on a rollercoaster ride and again, he looked at Hope, calm and serene, smiling her almost impeccable teeth. Being young was definitely the way to go.

The aircraft landed on the northerly runway and he saw the odd-style control tower, small by comparison to Glasgow's, tiny if you held it next to Edinburgh's. As the aircraft taxied in to the apron, the control staff waved to the plane—two men, one with headphones on.

Inside the terminal, he saw a man holding a sign with "Macleod / McGrath" written on it. On approaching him, Macleod's hand was grabbed and shaken forcibly before their bags were taken from them. It was explained that they were waiting for another guest before the trip continued and the man showed them to a seat and offered something from the airport cafe. Macleod refused and asked where the car would be as he fancied a walk.

The man shook his head. "Helicopter, sir, to the estate. I'll put your bags in the helo. Our other guest is expected in thirty minutes, so can you be here then and I'll take you to the helicopter?"

Macleod nodded and walked out of the terminal building. As he exited, he looked back at his partner who was talking to the man who had met them. She had his full attention and was conversing in a light way, playing with her hair as she did it. *Well he did have a helicopter*, thought Macleod, but it was just Hope being Hope.

Outside was cold and he walked through the snow on the pavement in his black shoes, thankful it was not any deeper than at present, lest his feet become chilled or wet. After the morning flights, the airport was starting to quieten down and he stood looking at the red vehicle trundling up and down the runway, stopping occasionally. The man driving the vehicle got out from time to time and fired a flare into the air which then dropped before exploding, sending a loud crack around the airfield. Once, a large flock of geese took to the air.

The sun broke through but it was still windy. Macleod looked at the towering clouds that seemed to pass down either side of the airfield and hoped they did not pass straight over, for there were showers of hail and snow underneath. Then he saw a small jet aircraft landing on the runway and heard Hope calling him.

"That's our other guest. Come back inside for a moment and he says he'll get them and introduce them to us."

Once inside Macleod felt the warmth return to his cheeks and looked at the entrance from the main apron, eagerly awaiting his companions for the next few days. He hoped they were not boring old business people rabbiting on about their wealth. He was not an easy listener.

Macleod was looking the wrong way as the pilot entered from the main doors with an airport representative and two young people, well young to Macleod anyway. The first was a tall, black man who seemed in the shape of his life. Macleod placed him about twenty-five and he wore a smart suit, the trendy sort Macleod would never be able to wear with confidence. His shoes gleamed and he wore a stylish hat to boot, a feather even extending from it. Beside him was a petite young girl, maybe very late teens, early twenties, with blonde hair that was held in a ponytail. Again, she had an athletic body and was dressed in smart blouse and trousers, although this hardly gave the fashion statement the credit it deserved.

"Well everyone, let me do some introductions," announced the pilot. "This is Detective Inspector Macleod and Detective Constable McGrath, from Police Scotland. And this is . . ."

"Aldo Brace and Zara Dawson," said Hope. "It's a pleasure to meet you both, and it's Hope and Seoras, we're not on official business after all. You guys just got together a month or so ago?"

"Yes," said Zara, "finally got my man."

"I do like a rugby player," said Hope, "and an international like Aldo Brace, wow, you did good, girl!"

Macleod felt Hope was being very forward and just who were these people and why did she know them? He enjoyed rugby on occasion too, but an American? He didn't know any American rugby stars. Were there such things? *I mean, Gavin Hastings, yes, Weir and the rest. But Aldo Brace? Never heard of him.*

"Good to meet you, Inspector," said Aldo reaching for Macleod's hand before crushing it in the strongest handshake Macleod had ever endured.

"Seoras, just Seoras," said Macleod. "It is a pleasure although I can't say I'm as au fait with modern sports as Hope is, do forgive me? Shouldn't you be at training or that sort of thing? I'm sure the season is well underway if you play in Europe."

"Injured and out for three months, Seoras."

"Lucky for me," said Zara and Macleod thought her smile would start to break the walls it was so large.

"Do you know our guests?" asked Hope.

"No, not really, but my agent said it would be a good idea, so here I am," replied Aldo.

"And where he goes, I go too," said Zara.

The pilot indicated it was time to go and led the small party down to a small apron opposite the control tower. It looked like something from World War II and Macleod saw the lime green paint flaking at the edges. He remembered the buildings he had seen around the airfield and how they were all green, hidden from the sky. Although these days, it was all commercial flights, but he felt good the past was still here, a side rarely told when he was growing up.

They were led to a small helicopter and fastened in the rear, while Aldo sat alongside the pilot in the front. As they departed the airfield, Macleod saw the Coastguard Rescue Helicopter sitting on its apron north of the large green hangar on the east side of the airfield. He was aware Zara was watching him stare at it.

"You ever seen one of those in action?" she asked.

Macleod stayed silent so Hope responded. "Yes, very impressive."

"They are that," said Macleod. "But I've seen them too often." The helicopter departed across the airfield and routed by the harbour. Looking out of the window Macleod saw the spot that came to mind at least once a day. *I've never forgotten you, my dear, I'm still sorry.*

Chapter 02

The helicopter raced over the white landscape which was interspersed with warm roofs that had driven off the snow. Macleod knew they were bound for Harris and one of the estates on that side but he realised that they had initially routed via the east coast of Lewis before cutting across somewhere around Scalpay. Tarbet, the town containing the ferry port that served the route to Skye, looked like a picture postcard. There were many good memories about the islands that he had forgotten over the years.

A large estate house reared up from the landscape and the small burn running down its eastern flank was the only non-white surface in sight. But there was a ring of orange in the snow with a large "H" in the snow and the pilot made straight for it. In front of it, a man wrapped up like a duvet waved his arms. Once the helicopter had landed, Macleod and company were ushered off and taken to the front of the house and through a set of large pillared doors. Inside, the air was warm and Macleod looked around wooden walls with large paintings and impressive tapestries.

A man bounced into the hall, dressed in a kilt and jacket, and took each of the new arrivals by the hand, shaking it vigorously.

"David Macaulay at your service. Delighted you got here; we were worried about the storms and whether the helicopter would make it. And the roads are such a pain, so it's good you're here. I hope you're all ready for some fun."

The man had curly ginger hair and Macleod reckoned he was a promotional figure for the tourist industry as his accent sounded like that one you hear on the television. The one every Scottish native grimaces at as no one here ever speaks like that. He was probably in his sixties and Macleod's boss had said the man was a publishing magnet, a man of serious money. She had no idea why she had been invited but circumstances had meant she was unavailable. So she had sent Macleod and McGrath because of their notoriety after the murders in Lewis. The man had been delighted apparently.

"And you must be Inspector Macleod. Magnificent work up in Stornoway. We don't have that sort of nonsense too often here on the islands so to clear it up was well done. You're a man from Lewis as well, I gathered. Great to have you here! You're ideal for what I have in mind."

"What do you have in mind?" asked Macleod. If there was a lack of enthusiasm he certainly was not hiding it. He'd left Jane for this and he hadn't been too happy about that.

"You'll see! Oh and Detective McGrath. Incredibly brave, holding that girl up in the water. And she made it because of you."

"Because of both of us, sir. We are a team."

"Indeed," said the man, "but you are the better-looking part, if I may say so, and no doubt, a lot of the brains as well. And Mr Brace, an honour, sir. We have covered you in our pages so often. And you bring me Miss Dawson, too. Such a delight, you really are the perfect showbiz couple. So delighted to have

16

you here." The man looked around for something, then bolted out of a nearby door before hurrying back through.

"Good, good. Kyle has your bags and will take you to your rooms. I wasn't sure about whether you needed separate rooms or not," he said looking at the younger pair, "so there's enough made up if you each require your own. In your rooms you, will find fine attire that I request you wear and then join me downstairs in the library room. It's through this door here and then two more. I'm sure you'll find it without problem and, if not, Kyle will round you up."

A woman entered via the main doors and whispered something in Macaulay's ear. He nodded and then held the woman's arm before she could depart. "This, my friends, is Mrs Smith, my housekeeper. She will attend to any needs you have and her son Kyle is our cook. Trust me, he's on the way up so you will enjoy sumptuous food. But I digress and we need to hurry lest we start late. So please, kindly to your rooms and I will await you in the library. Dress well, my friends."

The man bounded back out of the door he had come in and left the guests feeling somewhat disorientated. Seizing the situation, Mrs Smith asked if everyone would follow Kyle and stood with a look on her face that indicated that disobedience would be severely punished.

Macleod looked around him, ignoring Hope's raised eyebrows, and was the last to climb the wooden staircase behind their guide. The house had at least three floors and it was to the very top floor that the guests were taken. A great landing led off to many rooms and Macleod waited with Hope while Kyle showed Aldo and Zara their room. When he swept out of that room, Macleod struggled to follow Kyle who immediately opened up the room opposite announcing it was a perfect delight for any couple.

"Sorry, Kyle, but we're not together," said Macleod, "Partners, yes, but not together."

Kyle looked bemused and Hope assisted. "Colleagues, Kyle, work colleagues, nothing more. You see he's just not interested." Kyle raised his eyebrows before asking Macleod if he would wait in the room while he showed Hope to her own room. He took several pieces of clothing from the room as well and Macleod was left alone.

The room had a stunning four poster bed and was decorated in a classic style that would have suited the roaring twenties. But despite the charming lampstand and covered armchair, there were also some very modern conveniences, such as the large screen television and music system. Macleod saw USB ports on the wall. And yet there was a small door leading to an en-suite that screamed of a day gone by. The toilet seemed to have a classic chain to pull but when looking closer, Macleod saw the modern manufacturer's name on the cistern.

Making his way back inside, he took his small case and unpacked. Space for clothing was at a premium with the period wardrobe and dresser. Macleod carefully arranged his shaving gear and then sat down in the armchair. It was a sturdy piece of furniture, made with care by a real chair maker. He could sit here for hours if he had a good book.

Macleod was not investigating his room but instead was trying to stop himself from looking at the clothing on his bed—the clothing left for him by his host. As soon as the idea of a game had been announced, or at least a type of fancy dress, Macleod was appalled. He was too old for this sort of tomfoolery, especially when he could be at home with his Jane. Nonetheless, a curious eye now started to glance at the bed.

He saw a dapper suit and hat, one with a broad peak and he immediately was taken back to those classic black and white films. This could have been worn by Humphrey Bogart in *The Maltese Falcon*. There was a large trench coat as well, and he recognised this as the look of a sleuth. There was a card sitting on the bed which had the name on it crossed out and his own name written in delicate handwriting. So, this was meant for the boss's husband.

There came a knock at the door and Macleod gratefully answered it rather than get changed. Hope stood in slacks with a cream blouse and pair of simple heels on. Thick black glasses were on her nose and Macleod noted they were positioned so she could look over them. Like anything she wore, it looked good on her but this was not a sassy look, rather one of competence.

"And just who do they want you to be?" asked Macleod.

"A cultured librarian. Can't you tell? Looks pretty swish, if you ask me. But why are you not changed? This sounds like fun."

"If there's whisky I might take up drinking, Hope. What is this nonsense? The boss has a lot to answer for. She's ducked this deliberately."

"What did they give you?" asked Hope, marching past Macleod and lifting the clothing off his bed. "Wow, now this will look good, trust me, you're going to rock this. You've got that Sam Spade look about you anyway."

Macleod glowered at Hope. She was winding him up and he knew it. But she did it smiling all the time and with those engaging eyes that meant anyone would struggle to get annoyed with her. It was obvious this was her sort of thing.

"I'm going to powder my nose and then you shall meet me

19

outside my room. Don't keep a lady waiting."

"You know I'm the boss here," said Macleod, holding the door open for Hope.

"At times," said Hope, grinning as she left.

Macleod went to his en suite and washed his face. Getting up early was something for younger people. Or maybe it was the late nights. Whoever said that older people don't require as much sleep was a liar. Taking out his wash bag, Macleod squirted some shaving foam on his face and then delicately removed it with his razor. He hadn't shaved that morning and despite the fact he hardly sported any stubble, he still felt the need to be clean.

He dressed in the provided outfit and stood by the long mirror in his room. He thought he might be considered a handsome figure. The suit did look good and a detective from an older age was definitely looking back at him. He tipped the hat forward slightly. Well, if he was to partake in this charade he might as well try and enjoy it. No doubt the plot of whatever was about to happen—and he believed there would be a mystery otherwise why have detectives—would be puerile.

A knock came at the door and he called at the person outside to enter. Hope strode in and gave a wolf whistle.

"Told you! I knew you would rock that."

"Any idea what this is really all for?" asked Macleod.

"Some detective you are, haven't you read the card on the side?" said Hope.

"No, I was shaving."

"Beauty before business, eh?" She looked over her glasses at him and he admired the view.

"There might be some big spenders here," Macleod said to Hope. "You might strike it lucky. Take home a billionaire."

"My private life is none of your affair," she said sweeping in front of the mirror. "But you are right, I look hot. Surprised Jane let you away with me."

Macleod glanced up and saw the cheeky smile. He knew Hope was not so vain and the tease in her eyes brought a smile to his face.

"Good job she trusts me."

"Trusts me more like," said Hope. "Come on, let's get this party started. They'll be wanting to serve lunch soon, I guess. It's nearly twelve o'clock."

Macleod glanced at his watch. *A quarter past eleven. Hope must be hungry,* he thought. With that he held out his arm and let her attach herself to him.

"Did they give out any keys for the rooms?" asked Macleod. "Or did I just miss that?"

"Yes, you did, but really, what do you have with you to steal? Come on."

Macleod's wallet and mobile phone were on his person and so he reckoned that Hope was right. Shutting the door behind him, he escorted Hope down the flights of stairs and found the door leading through to the library. On entering, he saw a large number of people in period dress and his host standing at the far end of the room. The man stood up on a chair and banged a small glass with a spoon.

"Ah, our detectives have arrived, so let's begin."

Chapter 03

"Forgive me for standing on the furniture, my friends, but it will make it a little easier for you all to see. First, may I give a warm Harris welcome to our estate, one of the biggest in the area and purchased two years ago by myself. I have not been disappointed."

David Macaulay smiled broadly and basked in the appreciation of his enormous wealth. Scanning the room, he seemed to take a moment to survey the gathered throng.

"You may be wondering what I have planned for this weekend. Most of you know me on a business level, or at least know who I am. None of you have so far been included in my inner circle of friends, not deliberately excluded, of course—it's just that we haven't met. But I have gathered you here for a particular reason. You see, there is a problem with this house."

Macleod had been staring at the books on the many shelves of the library and had been generally bored at the proceedings so far. However, on hearing of a problem his interest was piqued. Turning and looking directly at his host, he saw the man start to frown. The man was still dressed in his kilt and jacket, but it was of an older cut, not so modern.

"You see, my friends, some say this place is haunted, but

I disagree. It is more than a haunting, it is something else coming through from beyond, maybe from a different region of space or time. We have had strange happenings in this house . . . presence of other things felt, objects moved, and people disappearing. I have informed the local police but they think I'm a crack pot. That's why I needed some of the country's top detectives."

No, no, no! Not a star turn, thought Macleod. *It's going to be one of those stupid homemade mysteries that doesn't really work and they'll try to make me look like an arse.*

"Inspector Macleod and the delightful Detective McGrath from Glasgow. They were the lead detectives in the murder cases in Lewis and the Black Isle. The best, I'm assured by the Chief Constable."

Well that's rubbish for a start, thought Macleod, *when did the Chief Constable ever come to see me!*

"I only hope you can help me, detectives. The rest of you have gathered for your expertise in your fields, along with your companions of course. I shall introduce everyone," continued Macaulay.

He jumped down from his chair and the gathering parted into a circle with Macaulay at the centre. He reached forward and grabbed a bald-headed man who seemed rather reticent to being manhandled. He was dressed in a long coat with green trousers and a white shirt underneath. Macleod thought his outfit to be that of a painter of days long gone.

"This, as I am sure we all know, is Mr Peter McKinney, who may be small in stature but who has shaken the art world to its core with his dynamic portrayal of everyday life in our fair country. His ability to reproduce the essence of his subject is beyond reproach. And he will help us by capturing the true detail of our encounters, for you see, these creatures cannot be captured with modern devices."

Peter McKinney looked at Macaulay as if he was mad but was joined at his side by a blond-haired, chunky man, who was wearing a tailored suit similar to Macleod's but without a hat.

"I'm Andrew but you can call me *Pandie*. I'm Peter's partner, married recently now that the law finally allows it. One more blow for the cause."

Macaulay looked a little taken aback by this interruption but he rallied superbly and shook Pandie's hand. "Delighted to have you with us. What special skills do you bring to the task, sir?"

Macleod nearly burst out laughing so engaged was Macaulay with the whole drama. He felt Hope elbow him and decided his face must be exhibiting his amusement just a little too much.

"Well, I'm a chef," said Pandie.

Macaulay was a little underwhelmed by this response. "Always good to have extra muscle on the side of goodness," said the host. "And speaking of muscle, we have two great athletes with us, Mr Aldo Brace and his stunning partner, Zara Dawson. No doubt we will have need of people who can crawl, climb, and generally deal with awkward places we need to investigate. So good to have our American friends with us."

Aldo nodded and smiled politely while Zara just beamed on his arm. Dressed in a pair of trousers and a light jumper, she cut a delightful figure, looking like a recent graduate from school, or so Macleod thought. Aldo was dressed in a suit, complete with handkerchief in his jacket pocket and a rose in the opposite lapel.

As the host sought his next victim, the wind suddenly howled outside and, looking through the window, Macleod saw the snow start to fall heavily. There were great white flakes that were being whipped here and there by the storm and he reckoned this fall was going to settle in heaps.

"Even the elements are against us, ladies and gentlemen. Do not be mistaken, we are up against elder creatures and foes from beyond. And that is why we need someone who can see through the lies and find the truth of what these gods are. So, I have called on the expertise of Jermaine Johnston, prominent atheist and regular battler with the religious authority in this land."

A small rotund man was brought into the centre of the gathering. He eyed Macleod suspiciously and got a distant look in return. The man was dressed in a white smock and sandals, clearly inappropriate for the setting. *But then again, this was a game and the figurines on the board had to look the part, did they not?* thought Macleod.

The man was joined by a large woman, possibly in her sixties and slightly older-looking than the man. She wore a large tartan shawl over tartan trousers, and Macleod thought she looked ridiculous.

"And Professor Christine Johnston, expert on ancient languages. Your linguistic skills will no doubt proffer us solutions we would otherwise struggle with."

The woman looked over a pair of small spectacles and frowned. "I doubt these languages will be much of a challenge."

"That's the spirit," said Macaulay. "We need to embrace these tasks before us. And may I also introduce my daughter, Lorraine, social expert and light of my life."

A woman stepped forward wearing an evening dress, light blue in colour and with a string of pearl beads around her neck. These were accompanied by a fur and white gloves. Macleod overheard a whisper, but he could not place the voice, "Trumped up TV parasite!"

"She's joined by her partner . . ." Macaulay hesitated briefly. "Anders Karlsen, bodyguard of many years."

The man was in a military uniform and Macleod almost laughed at it. It looked too formal, too many medal ribbons. But Anders was fronting up and playing the part. Together the air looked almost comical as Lorraine was petite and dark haired whereas Anders was well over six foot and blonde, giving the strangest match Macleod had seen in a while. He caught Hope's eye and she nodded in agreement. Strange!

"And lastly, let me introduce a woman of the world, one who understands the intentions of people the world over. She has dealt with the high and mighty, living the last five years in Russia and travelling all over the Asian continent." Macaulay took the hand of a blonde-haired woman dressed in a red evening gown with a large slit down one side that exposed a bare leg. "Everyone, this is Melanie Blayney, a Welsh goddess. I think you'll agree."

Macaulay's eyes were all over the woman who could only have been twenty-five at the most. Her dress, unlike that of Lorraine Baxter, was cut daringly and her ample cleavage was on display. Macleod heard the dissenting voice again and pinned it to Pandie.

"He's brought her here for the after-hours episodes then."

Ignoring the stage whisper, Macaulay waved to the doorway where Macleod saw his housekeeper, Mrs Smith, who was holding a tray of whisky glasses and walked around the guests dispersing the drinks.

"Raise a glass, everyone, to our endeavour; may we all keep

our minds—and our bodies—intact!"

Macleod threw his whisky into a plant pot as the rest toasted. At least this would all be over soon, but he was beginning to agree with Hope; lunch needed to be served.

"Now, let us sustain ourselves before we are to our task. Come friends—join me in the dining hall for a light lunch." And with a swish of his kilt and an arm on the sassy Melanie Blayney, David Macaulay led his assembled guests along a picture-strewn corridor and into one of the finest dining rooms Macleod had ever seen.

The room had panelled walls and long drapes, and looked out onto the estate beyond. The weather had turned the view an almost complete white but, here and there, a brave straggle of heather sprung through the blanket of snow. At the far end of the hall, a fire was ablaze that Macleod thought the Glasgow fire departments would struggle to douse. But its warmth was welcome when he looked outside where the blizzard of white continued to swirl.

A ringtone sounded out and Macleod saw Macaulay snap his fingers. Mrs Smith, the housekeeper appeared at one of the doors to the great hall holding a small basket that looked delicate. She walked towards the guests and then simply stood holding it out towards everyone.

"We have no need for mobile devices during our time. As I said, these beings that haunt the place cannot be captured with them so kindly leave your devices in the basket. My housekeeper will attend to all calls and contact you if the situation is urgent."

"Is it really necessary?" asked Aldo, "I could really do with posting a few things to Instagram. Keep my followers happy."

"My apologies, but yes. It's only for a day or so. But we must be focused, I'm sure you understand," said Macaulay.

Macleod looked at Hope. "Not sure about this," he said. "We really should be on the end of a phone."

"And we are," replied Hope. "Give them the house number and the housekeeper can come get us. I'm sure they won't mind. Signal's not great here anyway."

"An excellent suggestion Miss McGrath, as I would expect from a sensible upholder of the law like yourself," said Macaulay. "Mrs Smith, please take Miss McGrath to one of the house telephones so she can make that call. If that's okay with yourself, Inspector?"

Macleod nodded and then popped his mobile into the basket. It was lined with satin, or at least that's what Macleod guessed it was. A smell of barbequed meats then hit his nostrils and he saw a row of trenchers on tables at the far wall. Kyle Smith, dressed in his cook's whites, was opening the trenchers up and various smells were filling the air. Macleod's stomach grumbled. Breakfast was so long ago.

Macleod took a plate and filled it up with chicken, beef, pork, and some side dishes that he was unsure of. Taking a seat at the side of the hall, he was joined by Pandie McKinney, who sat down with aplomb. Macleod tucked into his food and became acutely aware he was being watched by the man beside him.

"I'm sorry, but is my plate that interesting?" he asked.

"Well, now that you ask," replied Pandie, "you have so much meat on the plate along with those vegetarian mains as well. Such a weird combination."

"Vegetarian mains?"

"Yes, the leeks in pastry, the aubergine, the butternut squas . . ."

"Side dishes. They are side dishes."

"Really, Inspector, or shall I call you . . . actually what is your first name?"

"Macleod!"

"It's Seoras," interjected Hope, returning to the hall.

"Your boss seems to like his vegetarian food," said Pandie.

"Just side dishes," grumbled Macleod, downing some more on a loaded fork.

Hope laughed. He's been brought up on meat and two veg," she said, "if you know what I mean."

"Indeed, I do!" replied Pandie, eyebrows raised. Macleod reckoned there was a double entendre there, but could not see it for the life of him.

"Don't I know you from somewhere?" asked Hope.

"Well, I always mix in the circles of the good-looking so, yes, you probably do."

"No, that's not it," said Hope. "A march. In Glasgow. I've seen your face, with a megaphone strapped to it." Hope raised her hand to her chin, deep in thought. "Gay pride march? No, gay rights march of some sort."

"Probably. You didn't arrest me, did you?"

Macleod looked at the man and then turned back to his food.

"Your boss not for everyone's rights."

Hope tried to take the answer, but Macleod was already up and ready to answer.

"I'm for everyone's rights. And responsibilities. But everyone has to shout and then fight. Gay rights, liberal rights, conservative rights, churches, the lot of you. And those climate warriors. Hours of police time wasted when we have a country to protect. It's as bad as the football."

Macleod saw Pandie about to respond when he suddenly stopped. Looking to his side, he saw Hope shaking her head at the man, advising him to stop.

"I've said my piece. Mr McKinney is entitled to his say. No offence intended, sir, but protests are a burden we don't need."

"But sometimes you have to protest. People have rights."

"I know. I uphold them." And the conversation died.

"Food looks good," said Hope.

Chapter 04

After the lunch, the guests were taken into a large drawing room, again with another enormous, roaring fire. It seemed to be a feature of the house and Macleod was glad of it. Outside, the wind was growing ever stronger and the snow continued to fall. When Macleod dared to look out of the large windows, complete with an old-style sash, he could barely identify the driveway of the house. There was a post which had grown wider with a packing of white on one side. And everything was so bright.

Once everyone had been served a drink, and Macleod had located himself near a generously proportioned plant, Macaulay announced it was time to begin the investigations. He asked everyone to find a comfortable position facing the fire. Once the general murmuring of people adjusting themselves had died down, Macaulay made his way to a switch and turned the lights off. The figure of Mrs Smith was then seen racing along the windows and pulling the drapes shut so the room was briefly left in darkness. There was the whir and Macleod saw the painting above the fire start to rise up and reveal a television set into the wall. The screen flickered to life.

"They walk among us" was the legend displayed on the

television before the picture cut to Macaulay standing outside a barn. He began rabbiting on about finding evidence of creatures coming to the House and its grounds, invading the Macaulay Estate and causing damage to fixtures and fittings. There was then talk of Great Old Ones and minions of some sort left on earth. Images of foreign cultures worshipping gods of various descriptions were shown including a lot of tentacles.

Macleod stared down at his whisky and poured another drop into the plant pot. He had switched off entirely from the presentation on the screen and was starting to watch the gathering around him. Along from him, Aldo Brace and Zara Dawson were standing hand in hand watching the screen. Sitting beyond them was Lorraine Baxter with her partner, Anders Karlsen, looking somewhat bored in a seat beside her. Macaulay was hopping from one foot to the other as he watched the screen while Melanie Blayney was standing just behind him, one hand on his neck rubbing it gently. But her eyes were on Miss Baxter. She was sizing up the daughter of the host.

Melanie's eyes flicked up and she stared at Macleod. She threw a cheeky smile and turned sideways while not breaking the stare. One bare leg snaked out and her eyebrows raised. Macleod looked away. But something in him was intrigued. Not by her physical charms which she was readily displaying, but in that face before she had been spotted. He waited a few moments and then snatched a glance back at Miss Blayney. Once more, she was staring at Miss Baxter.

Macleod looked away and began to scan the remainder of the room while the show continued. Everyone was staring at the television. Hope had glided silently around to him and was now whispering into his ear.

"That plant of yours is having a great time. Just be careful not to get it too pissed."

Macleod smiled an acknowledgement as the image of a tentacled being filled the screen and the screams of a woman were heard. Several of the guests jumped despite the sound clearly coming from the television.

"And so that is what we are here to investigate," announced Macaulay. Macleod had no idea what it was. Monsters, tribes, barns? *Oh well*, he thought, *I'll just have to wing it through the day. I expect dinner will be good.*

Macaulay was clearly in his element and Macleod was worried the man might wet himself such was the excitement on his face. With every moment, he was grinning at his guests and urging them into his fantasy world. Macleod was unsure how many were convinced. As he poured more whiskey into the now paralytic plant, he found his name being mentioned with others. He was being placed into a group, and more alarmingly, he was being sent to an outdoor barn. It looked cold out there. Daylight had flooded the room after the short presentation, Mrs Smith reprising her role and opening the drapes. It was wild out there.

Macaulay had split the group into three. Macleod was to be with Miss Baxter, Miss Blayney, and Jermaine Johnston, the man introduced as an atheist. Hope was to go with Macaulay, Peter McKinney, Mrs Johnston, and Aldo Brace. Anders Larsen, Zara Dawson, and Pandie were the last group.

As everyone mingled briefly before they departed to the various locations their little groups had been given, Hope breezed up to Macleod.

"Upstairs attic for me. Better than your expedition to the

frozen barn." She was laughing but he was not amused.

"It looks bitter out there," complained Macleod. "I hope they have some sort of overcoat I can wear." As if he was somehow overheard, Mrs Smith appeared at one of the doors with an array of coats for those "going outside". Macleod threw on a heavy trench coat and tried to pull his hat even tighter to his head. Macaulay came up to him, still bouncing about like a spring chicken, and slapped him on the side.

"At least, you've had plenty of the good stuff to keep you warm." Macleod nodded politely but could not help a surreptitious glance at the nearest plant pot.

"I believe I'm with you, Inspector," said a voice behind Macleod. He turned around and saw the delicate frame of Lorraine Baxter. He suddenly recognised her as the woman from the TV, one of those women's programmes that Jane had been watching. But she looked less plump in person. In fact, she was on the thin side of healthy.

"I believe so, Miss Baxter. Although I am not looking forward to stepping out into that storm outside.' The windows rattled as if to make Macleod's point for him and he saw Miss Baxter shiver slightly.

"I know what you mean, but father will be father." She started to wrap herself in a fur coat, provided by Mrs Smith and then gathered the rest of the small party.

"Macleod." Before Macleod stood Jermaine Johnston with his white smock on beneath the great overcoat he now wore. It was like a massive grey blanket on the short man and Macleod noticed he was still wearing his sandals.

"Johnston," Macleod replied. It was all he was getting after a curt introduction. And besides, Miss Blayney had arrived, wrapped in a raincoat. She looked extremely alluring, despite

the ordinariness of the coat and her infectious smile coupled
by her Welsh accent was sure to put many admirers on edge.

"Inspector, delighted to meet you. I love a man in uniform."
The statement came with a half wink and a shake of the hair,
that was not unappreciated by Macleod. But he was still wary
of her earlier study of Miss Baxter and decided he needed to
steer clear of Miss Blayney's charms.

"It's Seoras, please, all of you, call me Seoras. And I haven't
been in uniform for some time. I believe we are to head
outside now, so shall we? I think we should escort the ladies,
Mr Johnston. If you would take my arm Miss Baxter, I'll be
delighted to strike out first into this melee of white that awaits
us."

Miss Baxter took his arm rather gratefully. Maybe she was
not that impressed with Mr Johnston. Together they walked
out of the room, along several corridors and then through a
rear entrance. The door fought hard not to open and Macleod
stood up against it to let the others through. With one hand
on his head and his other now around Miss Baxter's shoulder,
he steered towards the barn finding his feet disappearing up
to his ankles at times.

Before them stood a large barn with a single door crashing
in the wind. The snow was lying right up to the door and
Macleod saw little of the surroundings such was the heaviness
of the falling snow. Again, he stood at the entrance making
sure the door did not move and ushered his small team inside.
Once all were accounted for, Macleod stepped inside himself
and shut the door quickly.

"It's dark," said Miss Blayney. "Don't try anything, Mr
Johnston." A grunt was the only reply.

Macleod tried to pull his pen torch from his pocket but

realised that he had left it with his normal clothing. His eyes peered into the blackness and after a few moments, when they were becoming accustomed to the lack of light, he managed to spot a small, old fashioned lantern. Reaching down, he found a packet of matches beside it. Opening the lantern, Macleod adjusted its settings and then lit it. A soft glow came out that struggled to penetrate the darkness.

"Well done, Seoras," said Miss Baxter, "and do call me Lorraine." She stepped close to him and took his arm. Mr Johnston stood just inside the door looking unamused while Miss Blayney tried to take Macleod's other arm.

"I'm sorry, Miss Blayney; with Miss Baxter on one arm, I'm afraid I need the other to operate the lantern. Maybe Mr Johnston will give you his arm again."

"Back home, a man never refuses two women at once," said Miss Blayney. "And it's Melanie, although you can call me Mel if you wish, Seoras. My last lover called me Mel—I quite enjoyed it."

Macleod was not sure what the woman was implying and so ignored the additional comment. Instead, he stepped forward with Miss Baxter and began to search the room with the small lantern. He was sure he felt her grip tighter as they stepped further into the dark.

The barn was wooden in construction and the dim light showed a mezzanine level which seemed to contain hay of some type. A ladder ran up to it. The sides of the barn had various hand agricultural items, such as a scythes, sickles, and pitchforks. The floor was concrete and dusty. An old car sat in the middle of the barn and Macleod thought it must be from the thirties.

Something occurred to Macleod. He was investigating this

barn with no idea what he was looking for. He had drifted off during the talk on the purpose of the gathering. So much so, that he was totally lost on what they were doing and why. He tried holding back a little to see if Miss Baxter would start to steer their search but on stopping she simply stood beside him, nervous.

"Apart from the car, there's nothing in here," said Macleod. "At least there's nothing obvious. What is it we're looking for?"

"The cult would leave marks. Indicators for others who came after them, routes laid out to the chambers they use. Sacrificial areas, possibly holding pens, markings showing doorways." It was the first Jermaine Johnston had spoken and it was curt, giving the impression he was above everyone else. Macleod was taking a distinct disliking to the man.

"Can you see anything of note, Mr Johnston?" asked Macleod.

"No. But I'll need a closer look. I shall examine the car."

Macleod found his lantern taken off him and Miss Baxter gripping him even tighter. While Mr Johnston began to open the car, Miss Blayney walked to the edges of the darkness looking into the corners of the room.

"We'll need to look up where the hay is, too," said Miss Blayney.

"Obviously," came the curt reply from inside the car.

The silence in the barn made the noise of the wind and snow outside seem even louder. Occasionally, Mr Johnston would swear as he bumped his head or hand whilst searching and Macleod would grimace. Then the man emerged looking hot and flustered, which was impressive in such a cold barn.

"There's nothing bloody there."

"Did you search the glovebox? Under the seats?" asked Miss

Blayney.

"I could find an atom in a gnat's arse, dear. Of course, I bloody looked there."

"Then maybe you should check the mezzanine level," suggested Miss Baxter.

"Indeed, I shall. Maybe you would assist me, Inspector."

"Of course," replied Macleod, removing Miss Baxter's arm which was a process harder than he would have imagined. Macleod followed Johnston up the rickety ladder before climbing onto the floor above. There was hay everywhere. Johnston looked around and then started to fling hay here and there. There was such a randomness to his searching that Macleod felt the need to step in.

"Mr Johnston, let me. There are more sensible methods to these things." Not waiting for an answer, Macleod started at one side and began to shift hay to one side gradually unveiling the floor and sides piece by piece. As he moved one large bundle aside, he saw a design in the wall. It was ornate and seemed to have creatures with large tentacles on it. After a moment's contemplation, he was brushed aside by Mr Johnston who dropped to his knees before the symbol, muttering to himself.

"Have you found something?" asked Miss Baxter. "Do hurry; it's very dark down here."

"We have something. Mr Johnston is examining it," replied Macleod.

There was another two minutes of silence before an excited Johnston stood up and urged Macleod to uncover more of the hay. After ten more minutes of work there was nothing else to be found and the men descended the ladder.

"What was it?" asked Miss Blayney.

"A marking. A simple one but this is a place of meeting," said Johnston.

"Of the cult?" asked Macleod.

"Of course, of the cult. It's hardly the Mothers Union local branch. But there's nothing else. This must be a meeting place only. There's nowhere else to go." Johnston turned to go to the barn door.

"Hold up," said Macleod. "I'll give the car the once over, too. Two eyes are better than one."

Johnston groaned and shook his head. "If it will give you a smidgeon of satisfaction then by all means, Inspector." The man's contempt for the world was obvious.

Macleod took the lantern and saw the apologetic look on Miss Baxter's face. Climbing into the car, he made his way through all the nooks and crevices, opened everything that he could. Then he got out and checked the boot and the bonnet. Nothing unusual.

"You see, nothing at all, Inspector," said Johnston.

"Just a moment, please," came Macleod's calm reply. He got down on the floor and shone the light under the car. On standing up again, Macleod gave the lantern to Miss Baxter.

"Ah, good. You are complete, Inspector. Let us get back into the warmth of the house," said Johnston.

"Good idea," said Miss Blayney, "I could do with being warmed up." Her eyes were on Macleod as she said it and he couldn't help but feel a little uncomfortable. Something was not right with that woman.

"Are you complete, Seoras?" asked Miss Baxter.

"No," Macleod replied, "I'm not. Just a moment." Macleod reached inside the car again and released the handbrake and took the car out of gear. He then put his shoulder to the side of the car and began to slowly roll it forward. Looking over his shoulder, Macleod suddenly stopped the car.

"Very good, you moved a car; can we get back?" asked Johnston.

"Take the light behind the car, Lorraine," instructed Macleod.

Miss Baxter stepped gingerly behind the car and then suddenly dropped the lamp. She shrieked to the air as she turned desperately trying to find anyone else. Macleod lit a match.

"What is it?" asked Macleod.

"There, oh god, just there. Don't make me look."

Macleod walked over just as his match went out. He lit another one and located the lantern, setting it upright and relighting it. Then he turned to the floor behind the car. There was a picture on the floor of some kind of creature devouring a woman. The picture was gross but it was only a picture to Macleod. He'd seen some worse sights in his time. Although the vividness of the picture was stunning.

Johnston walked past Macleod and looked at the image. He was joined on the other side by Miss Blayney who didn't flinch at all. Macleod heard the grumblings of Johnston, probably annoyed that Macleod had got one over on him. But Macleod was about to go one further. He ran his fingers along the edges of the picture before standing and retrieving a pitch fork from the side of the barn. Carefully, he wedged it into the little crevice and worked the picture up. Johnston removed the image and they were left with a hole, barely man-sized, which led to a new darkness below.

"I guess we need to go down there," said Macleod.

"That bastard of a father of mine," said Miss Baxter, and she gripped Macleod's arm again. This time he was afraid she'd cut off the circulation.

Chapter 05

"I shall go down first," announced Mr Johnston and then knelt before swinging himself into the dark void. Macleod stood with the lantern above the descending man and could see what he thought was a floor below.

"There seems to be floor beneath, Mr Johnston. Are you okay to drop or do you want me to help lower you?" asked Macleod.

"I'm fine," insisted Johnston, and he dropped down whereupon a loud thud was heard followed by a yelp. Macleod quickly knelt down and stuck his head into the aperture, lowering the lantern in as well. On the floor, holding his knee and giving a strong grimace, was Mr Johnston.

"Are you okay, sir?" asked Macleod.

The man seemed to swear under his breath. "I think my knee has gone."

"What do you mean by gone?" said Miss Baxter from above.

"I think it has been jarred, Miss Baxter. I'm not sure how much weight I can put on it."

"If you give me your hand, sir, I'll pull you back up," said Macleod.

"Nonsense. I shall crawl if I have to. Besides, you shall need me if you are to solve anything."

Macleod at first felt indignant. *Need the man. I'm a Detective Inspector. I have solved a few mysteries in my time, the real kind. And so far, he has found nothing and wrecked his knee. Stupid arse.* But then Macleod began to smile, and fought hard to supress a laugh. The man was comical really.

"Fair enough. I shall come down with the ladies presently," said Macleod. "You first, Lorraine?"

"I don't want to go down there," she replied, giving a small shiver in the gloom. "It won't be pleasant. He's always wanted to do this sort of shit and he knows I hate it."

"You don't need to go down," said Miss Blayney. "Seoras has matches we can leave you with. We'll need the lantern of course."

"You're not leaving me up here alone. Lower me down, Seoras. I'll keep to the rear."

Miss Baxter was lowered through the hole, followed by Miss Blayney, before Macleod descended. The drop was only around six feet and Macleod wondered how Johnston had managed to injure himself. Holding the lantern, he took the lead and began to search in the darkness. Miss Baxter, who had wanted to remain at the rear, grabbed his arm again, clinging tightly. Behind them, Macleod heard Miss Blayney complaining about the shuffling Johnston, who was trying to force his way to the front despite his injury.

They were inside a concrete lined corridor. The walls were cold and damp to the touch, mildew present on all sides. Macleod did not want to touch the sides but Miss Baxter was determined to hang onto him which meant they were trying to move a two-person shape along a corridor built for maybe a person and a half. At least they weren't his clothes that were being covered with the powdery white spores.

The corridor seemed to run for an age, although they were probably only walking for about five minutes through the dark. As they continued, they started to hear voices, low at first before becoming distinctly audible. It was not any language Macleod knew but then again, that meant it was not Scots Gaelic or English.

"Dear God, did you hear that?" whispered Johnston. "They are performing a summoning. They are calling up some sort of creature."

"How can you tell that?" asked Miss Blayney.

"I'm well aware of my Latin, madam, and that was a sum-moning."

Macleod continued towards the sounds and even his heart was beating a little faster in the dark. It may have been a game, but it was an effective one. As he peered into the gloom, he saw a wooden door ahead, another symbol stamped onto it. More tentacles and writing in a language he could not understand.

"There's a symbol on the door," said Macleod.

"Let me through," whispered Johnston, fiercely. "This will require an expert."

The problem was there was nowhere to go for anyone and Macleod found himself pushed up tight to Miss Baxter while Johnston pushed past at about knee height, walking on one knee and his hands. Miss Baxter was petite and Macleod found he rather overwhelmed her figure leaving them in a tight embrace that was more appropriate for lovers rather than two thrown-together participants in a weird role-play. When Miss Blayney pushed up close to see the door as well, Macleod felt like he was in a crude-seventies British farce.

"There's a summoning room in there," said Johnston, excit-edly. "Definitely a place of worship and summoning."

"Devil worship?" asked Macleod.

"This is no children's fantasy of Jesus and the devil, sir. This is about the Elder beings that came from afar. And in there they seek to open a gateway."

Macleod struggled somewhat with having his own faith described as a fantasy as they were running around in costumes seeking made-up creatures. But he let it slide as he wanted to be free from the press he was now stuck in.

"Can you open the door?" he asked.

"I think so," said Johnston as the sounds of voices grew louder. There were chants now and someone yelling out in that language again.

"I don't want it open," shouted Miss Baxter and she flung her arms around Macleod. "I won't look," she continued and buried her head in Macleod's chest.

"We are opening it, madam," shouted Johnston and Macleod saw him turn a handle and the door opened up. Johnston shuffled through and Macleod managed to extract himself from Miss Baxter and tumble through the door along with Miss Blayney. The sight that was laid before him made him start.

The room was lit by several burning brands and there was a stone slab at the far end of the room. The walls had a multitude of symbology on them, intricate and full of those tentacles again. Outside of these adornments, the room was bare. Except for the blood and bodies.

Various body parts lay scattered around the blood-drenched room. At their feet ran a pool of red emanating from the head of something. The pointed ears and waxy reddish skin told Macleod it was not something human but that did not stop the revulsion he felt. As a good Detective Inspector should, he

45

made a very quick count of the bodies, eight, and scanned the room for anyone else. A door swung on the far wall and he saw footprints, several of them in damp blood, leading through the door. On instinct he ran across the room and charged through the door. There was a set of wooden steps which had bloody footprints on them. Racing up to them, he then found and opened a wooden door which allowed a wild wind and a blast of snow to assault his perspiring face. Before him, as he shielded his eyes from the storm, he was able to make blood disappearing for a short distance and then there was nothing.

The cold bit at him and he fought through the storm to the end of the red footprints. Beyond this there was nothing. As his heart pounded from the thrill of the chase and the scene he had just witnessed, Macleod found the voice of experience talking to him. *Stop, slow down. It's a game, there's nothing real here. Just walk back in; that's what you're meant to do. Play the game.*

Turning back, he was grateful to reach the wooden steps and be inside. The weather was brutal and he thought it was bad enough that if it continued it would cause serious problems to moving about. The timing of the whole show he had witnessed was remarkable. The sounds that came right on cue as they entered, the swinging door, and the bloody footprints out of the underground chamber all measured up to what was supposed to be going on. And yet it was a game.

Macleod bent down on the steps and dipped his hand into one of the small pools of blood. Licking it, he pondered the taste. It was sweet, to a point. It was not human blood, there was a lack of saltiness. No, it was probably pig's blood. He used to eat black pudding with this blood in it but in its current form, it seemed gross.

46

The crying from inside the underground room brought him out of his investigative sense and back to thinking about his companions on this exercise. As he walked back into the room, he saw Miss Baxter face on to a wall, rocking where she stood. Jermaine Johnston was crawling around, looking at the symbology on the walls and the glamorous Miss Blayney was standing over one of the heads on the floor.

Macleod walked over to Miss Baxter and placed an arm around her. "It's okay, they are all just fakes," he said. "All just part of the game."

The woman sobbed while Johnston barked, "No need to ruin it; keep in character, man."

"I know they're fakes," yelled Miss Baxter. "But it's bloody gross. He always pulls this crap, always."

"Your father has thrown these sorts of events before?" asked Macleod.

Miss Baxter turned and now held onto Macleod, burying her head in his chest. "Not on this scale," she sniffed. "But he's done it in a room without telling me, or just a one off. It's why he bought this place, to create a horror show."

"Please!" demanded Johnston, "Can we stay in the spirit of the thing? These are definitely elder markings I'm seeing, some form of cult worship. And the way they had decapitated these creatures, it's clearly a ritual killing. Let's look round the room and find some more clues. Obviously, if you find something, bring it to me as I'll need to examine it. I doubt you'll be able to contribute more than your physical efforts."

"We'll help once we have Miss Baxter in a place she wants to be, Johnston," said Macleod, as he scanned the woman, thinking he may have to take her back to the house. She was as white as the proverbial sheet and was still shaking despite gripping him like he was a winning lottery ticket.

"I'll be okay," said Miss Baxter. "Sit me in the doorway so I can still have the light and don't leave without me."

"Of course," said Macleod. "But I'll stay with you if you need company. It's okay, your well-being is the most important thing."

Miss Blayney came over and gave a little shiver. Macleod thought it was put on and watched the woman take off her coat and offer it to Miss Baxter. The trembling woman took it and Macleod sat her down in the doorway and watched her close her eyes. As he stood there, Miss Blayney placed a hand on his shoulder and leaned close into him. Macleod felt it inappropriate, especially when a whisper came into his ear.

"Leave the little scaredy-cat, Seoras. I could do with a man like you . . . to help look over this place. I'm sure you're used to noticing the finer details in life."

Macleod turned and Miss Blayney's face was up close. She flashed a cheeky smile and flicked her eyebrows to highlight the innuendo she had just used. Despite enjoying the attention of almost any woman who was flirting at him, Macleod was also not oblivious to the obvious attempt to garner something. He was just not sure yet what it was Miss Blayney wanted. She was stunning and her Welsh tone only added to her sexiness. But alarm bells were going off in his head.

Together with Miss Blayney, he helped look over the room. He picked up several of the decapitated heads in a fashion he never got to in the day job, for forensics would have torn him apart for contaminating a scene. Under one, he found a book with some strange symbols on it and a language inside he could not understand.

"Johnston," said Macleod, "I have a little light reading for you." On throwing the book to the man who was still shuffling comically around the room on his bottom, Macleod watched his face light up with glee. But Macleod did not hang about. He had a woman in a distressed state in the doorway and she needed to get back to the house. He knew what he wanted to know. The blood was pig, or at least animal, and having handled the heads and bodies, they were latex. It was all fake and even though he was not sure how the sounds were managed in such a perfect manner, there was no foul play here, all just a game. A pretty sick one though.

"Come on, Johnston, you can read that book back at the house. We've seen everything."

"We need to go over everything even closer," said Johnston. "Isn't it marvellous? We are actually in a cult ritual sacrifice. More time is required, Inspector."

"I'm going back," Macleod stated as a fact. "You can remain but I'm taking Lorraine to the house. She needs to lie down and maybe get a stiff drink. She's also frozen. Melanie, are you staying with Mr Johnston or coming with us?"

The Welsh bombshell made a beeline for Macleod and stood just a little too close to him. "Let's go Seoras. I could do with a hot shower."

She had said nothing provocative but Macleod found the way she talked about a shower somewhat alluring, as if she had made a pass at him. He shook a metaphorical head and focused on the problem at hand.

"You coming, Johnston, or will you be sliding on your bottom to the house on your own?"

Johnston swore but turned around and started to shuffle towards the door. Macleod watched him pass through the blood on the floor without even a sign of disgust. With an arm around Miss Baxter and Miss Blayney as close as a person could get in the small corridor, Macleod led the way back to the opening, using the lantern. Once there, he had to send the women up, Miss Blayney being the first to go. Macleod doubted she was the clumsy creature she made out to be as he lifted her on his shoulders. Her body seemed to fall and dip at awkward times, making it seem like he was in one of those Carry-On films.

Lifting Miss Baxter up afterwards was a simple affair, as the woman was petite but Johnston was something else altogether. Trying to get him to stand was bad enough but he rocked and complained which caused the figure of Macleod and himself, the latter on top of the former, to tumble and bounce off the wall more than once. The blood that had soaked around Johnston's bottom was also beginning to drip down Macleod's neck and so he hurried to get the man up into the barn.

He was then helped up by the women and the party made their way through the blizzard to the house. The progress was slow due to the shuffling Johnston and by the time they had arrived, their garments wore a side of snow. Macleod took Miss Baxter into the library room where the other parties had gathered on their return. Having made her comfortable in a large armchair, he made her a stiff brandy and then found himself a coffee.

"Are you alright?" asked Hope, entering the library.

"It's a bit weird, isn't it?" said Macleod.

"Too right, but wait until you hear what happened with my group."

Chapter 06

Having left Macleod at the dining room, Hope made her way with her host and the other two guests in her group up the main staircase of the house. The flights of stairs seemed to be causing Christine Johnston some discomfort and she complained all the way up. By contrast, Aldo Brace seemed to bound up them and had to wait several times for the rest of his group. Macaulay skipped along, like an excited child as they went up higher until they reached the top landing. From here he directed them to a ladder that was hanging out of the ceiling through an open closure.

"That's the attic, up there," said Macaulay. I've been up there once but when I saw the markings I made my way back down quickly. It's not a place you want to venture through alone, trust me."

Hope looked over her thick-rimmed glasses with a style she thought might be the thoughtful librarian. "Really, Mr Macaulay, you expect us to believe in these creatures you talk about. I'll gladly see your ideas debunked." Hope decided this was the sort of play along Macaulay was looking for and when she saw his smile followed by a look of horror, she knew she had pitched it right.

"Well, if the lady's for looking, can't have her go up alone," said Aldo Brace and took Hope's arm and led her to the ladder. "Should a gentleman go first on this occasion or would that be stifling your investigative longing?"

He's really going for it, thought Hope. *This could be good.*

"More ladders! Good God, Macaulay, are you trying to kill me?" snorted Mrs Johnston.

"I shall assist you, dear lady," said Macaulay, "but perhaps we should let the younger pair take the lead."

Hope stepped onto the bottom rung and began to climb the wooden ladder with Aldo then bracing it at the bottom. Her head poked up into darkness and she struggled to see anything.

"Is there a light switch near here, Mr Macaulay?"

"Yes, on your right, and first names please, Hope. It's David."

"Okay, David." Hope swept her hand to the right and at first moved across a bag. Then she found the switch, on the floor, or rather on a beam, and flicked it on. A flickering light came on and she scanned around the attic. There was junk everywhere. Boxes were stacked to the roof beams and across the floor Hope saw erratic boards that spanned the beams that held up the ceiling below.

"Okay, we're good. But it'll be a bit cramped. And David, I can't see anything weird or evil up here."

"It was further in," said David. "I shall show you but please be quiet in case we disturb anything."

The idea that they needed to be quiet was severely challenged when Christine Johnston came up the ladder, after taking over three minutes to climb the short fixture, she huffed and puffed in the cold attic. Macaulay followed her up the ladder and grinned broadly on arrival as the four of them were stuck in a small space.

"There, Christine, we are all up and ready to move on. But

be silent as we travel, hushed whispers only, lest we draw something to us."

"It's Mrs Johnston, Mr Macaulay, I'm not some young girl who enjoys being fawned over. And I need some room. You, the American chap, move over and let your elders have some space." Mrs Johnston's hips banged into Aldo Brace's side and he fell into Hope grabbing her shoulders to steady himself. Hope looked into the white eyes that looked shocked against his dark skin but then they both smiled at each other and broke into a giggle.

"Quiet," said Macaulay, but not too severely, "and lead the way, Hope. It was further along if you can find a path."

Steadying herself, Hope started along the attic and noticed a strong draft coming from the far end. It was sending a cold wind into her blouse making it flutter and she wished she had a coat. Aldo was not far behind her and she heard him shiver, too. It was like there was a gaping hole somewhere and the outside wind, which was audible on the floor below—although muted—was now streaming in. The light flickered still, making it hard for Hope to see as her body and that of her party blocked the poor patches of illumination that were making it this far along the attic.

Then before her Hope noticed that the attic had been disturbed. There was a grandfather clock sat on its side across the beams and boxes were strewn here and there. She focused on the floor and managed to straddle the clock to get access beyond but now it was becoming darker and she went onto her hands and knees to feel out the flooring. And the draught was getting stronger. A small patch of daylight could be seen in the beams and Hope thought she saw something move.

"Hold up," she said softly but loud enough to make herself

heard over the wind.

"What is it?" asked Aldo.

"There's something in the beams, maybe sitting in a gap in the roof. It's at least man-sized if not more."

Aldo came down close behind her and she pointed to the figure she was beginning to discern. Behind, she heard the fussing of Mrs Johnston as she crossed the grandfather clock with a little help from Macaulay.

"Dear God," said Macaulay suddenly, "I thought I saw a rat."

"Rat!" shrieked Mrs Johnston and bolted forward into Aldo who clattered into Hope on the floor. The noise echoed around the attic. Hope looked up as she tried to find her feet again and the figure in the attic roof was moving causing sunlight to flood into the space. She could barely make out the figure but swore she saw red eyes and wings as it seemed to swoop towards them in the small space. Hope raised her hands to defend herself as Mrs Johnston screamed. The creature was inches from them when the floor suddenly caved in.

Hope fell and lost her awareness of where she was going. She tumbled head first and landed with her hands first to strike something soft. With a deafening crash, she felt herself stopping, her body flipping over and settling on something gentle, almost relaxing, but there was powder everywhere. Or was it plaster? Her glasses had gone half-cocked and she reached up to adjust them before remembering the creature. As she looked up, she saw a hole in the ceiling and light pouring in above. Apart from the howling wind there was a brief silence.

"What in the name of God Almighty have you done to me, Macaulay?"

At least Mrs Johnston seemed alright. Hope rolled to one

side and found it difficult due to the softness of the boxes she had landed on. With hands and knees working overtime, she managed to extricate herself from the mess and stood on solid floorboards again. Above her the howl of the wind came through from above, chilling her.

Watching Mrs Johnston's efforts to get clear of the boxes made Hope feel a compassion for the woman, far above any she expected to have, and she helped her out with a strong hand to cling to. Macaulay desperately tried to control his kilt as he flashed enough thigh to have Hope seriously worried she might have to arrest him for gross indecency. Aldo Brace easily climbed out, being fitter and stronger than Hope.

"Well, what was that all about, Macaulay?" asked Mrs Johnston.

"It was one of the winged creatures I spoke about in the library. They come at me, as if this place is not mine but theirs. Like I am trespassing in this house."

Hope had tried to listen to everything Macaulay had said but the early start had lessened her enthusiasm and she could not recall the bit about the winged creatures. But it was all a bit of a laugh anyway, and she was still getting paid. She thought of how Macleod would be feeling though and chuckled inwardly.

"This is a part of the house I haven't been able to get to in months," announced Macaulay. "It used to be my departed mother-in-law's room. A strange woman and I had all her things removed when she passed on. She was a burden but then my dear departed wife would have wanted me to look after her, so I did. But she always said her mother would want her privacy. And that room," he said pointing to a large wooden door across from where they stood, "is one I have never entered into."

55

"How long have you had the estate," asked Hope.

"Three years and the woman perished after only one, cursing me for taking her from her previous residence."

"Which was where?"

"By the banks of the Miskatonic."

"In the USA?" queried Mrs Johnston.

"Yes, that's it, near the university."

"I've never heard of the Miskatonic," said Aldo Brace, "and I have travelled all over our great nation with my rugby. Never heard of it. Is it a New England place? I'm not too familiar with New England, if I'm honest."

Aldo smiled at Hope, fishing to see if he was being useful, she thought. For such an athlete, he certainly seems to have a lack of confidence when the talking starts.

"Look," said Macaulay, taking a photograph off the wall. "That's my wife's mother. Older there of course and unwell."

"What's wrong with her head?" asked Mrs Johnston.

"What do you mean?" asked Macaulay.

A firm finger pointed to the woman's cranium and then to the picture. "Observe, Macaulay. My head is round from above or reasonably close. Her head is elliptical. It's weird, positively strange. And she's nearly bald."

Hope nearly burst out laughing but was keen to keep up the pretence in her role-play and so let out a gasp. Her eye caught Aldo's and he nearly burst out laughing too.

"I don't know quite what happened but she changed. But she wanted a sea view—hence the window on the far side. If you look, you can see a bay down there, one that she insisted on seeing. She said it helped her see those gone before. Daft old bat, really."

"But what's behind the door?" said Hope. "What was she

56

hiding?" Hope tipped the glasses right onto the end of her nose and peered over them at her companions. "I think we should investigate, find out what she was doing up here."

Macaulay seemed to start skipping again, the spring in his step resembling a spring lamb. *I'm playing his game*, thought Hope.

"It has a lock," said Aldo, "maybe there's a key in amongst this junk somewhere."

The smile on Macaulay's face was too much to hide and Hope knew they were following the game correctly. But Mrs Johnston refused to trawl through the boxes, stating she had been through enough exertions and would rest while they looked. Aldo tore through the boxes and after ten minutes they found an old key on the floor, under a seemingly collapsed set of drawers.

"Okay, Aldo, open it," said Hope.

The rugby player gingerly placed the key in the lock and turned it. There was a click and then he slowly began to open the door. Inside was dark but the penetrating light from the connecting room allowed Hope to see there was a table in the middle of the room.

"Anyone got a match?" asked Macaulay, but they all shook their heads. "Looks like we'll need to be careful then," he said.

Aldo and Hope strode in and found a wooden table that held two glasses and two wooden plates. There was foul smelling, heavily decomposed food on the plate. She bent down and ran her hand along the table leg. Something felt strange. With a subtle hand, she surreptitiously lifted one side of the table, it weighed so very little, she nearly started to flip it.

"Look here," said Macaulay, pointing at a picture on the wall adjacent to the door they had entered. *Good distraction, I nearly blew one of your little gadgets there.* Hope turned her face impassively to the picture Macaulay was indicating.

"Why, there's a text on the scroll," said Mrs Johnston.

Hope looked at the picture. There was a man, hunched and misshapen, who was carrying a scroll. His head was like Macaulay's mother-in-law, elliptical. Beside him was a loch of water and something dark was rising from the water.

"What is it?" asked Aldo.

"The words are ancient Norse. Not my first specialty but words I am familiar enough with," said Mrs Johnston with pride. "For when they come from afar, they shall find a home at the waters of . . . damn, there's a tear right there. But there's more below. Look at the bottom of the picture." She stared intently, the rest of the party hanging on her words. "We bid you come from darkest night and rise once more. Great master of the sea and the one who has laid in darkest night, send your emissary to me!"

The door to the room suddenly slammed shut. A howling began from behind the group and they turned around to see the far wall begin to spin. The whole length of it span into a vortex that seemed to drag things toward it, the table and chairs beginning to slide. A wind blew from behind Hope and she found herself struggling to stand. Together they gripped each other as the furniture collapsed and then disappeared into the spinning vortex.

And then an arm crawled forward in the darkness. It was tentacled and grabbed Macaulay's leg. Hope tried to grab it but the spongy arm was too strong for her and Macaulay was dragged forward.

"Shut the portal," he yelled. "Shut it!"

Mrs Johnston was now looking at the picture again. "It's in

here somewhere, I know it," she said.

"Hold onto me, Hope, Aldo. I need you to hold onto me."

Hope grabbed Macaulay's hand and Aldo held the other one but the tentacle was still gripping onto his foot. The pull was powerful and they were slowly being dragged toward the vortex. The wind blowing through her hair made Hope feel alive and she was enjoying this. Her blouse rippled and she threw her head back, imagining herself on a 1960s horror film poster.

"For now is not your time, and to darkness you must wait, oh master of the sea and keeper of the deep; I bid you farewell."

As soon as Mrs Johnston had said the words, the arm released its grip and disappeared into the vortex. The room went dark and Macaulay could be heard getting to his feet. "Out!" he yelled, "For God's sake, get out, all of you."

The door opened courtesy of Aldo and the light allowed Hope to grab Mrs Johnston and steer her away from the chaos of the room. Once outside, Macaulay opened the other door in the room they had dropped into and they stumbled out onto a landing.

"Did we all make it?" asked Macaulay.

Very good, Mr Macaulay, very good! How did you make that all happen? But I don't really care, thought Hope; *this is bloody fantastic, just bloody fantastic!*

Chapter 07

The library room was abuzz with conversation about the ghastly sights that had been seen. The third group of Anders Karlsen, Pandie, and Zara Dawson were the subject of an encounter in the cellar and had found evidence of elliptical-headed people as well, including a diary written by one of them. Drinks were flowing as most people engaged in the mystery. But not Lorraine Baxter, who seemed to simply drink whisky at a rate a hard-nosed fisherman would have been proud of.

"What's up with her?" asked Hope.

"She's not really enjoying her father's pranks," replied Macleod. "There was a lot of blood at our venue, and it was real blood. Animal blood but real—probably pig."

"Did she have a bit of a breakdown?"

"More than a bit, Hope. A full pint of breakdown, complete with chaser."

In the meantime, Macaulay was racing from person to person, discussing what had happened. He spent considerable time with Mr Johnston who had thankfully changed his blood-soaked clothes but who was still as enthusiastic and arrogant. But he was being fed by Macaulay.

Pandie was also enjoying himself, and had emptied the best

part of a bottle of red wine. His partner, Peter McKinney, was sitting down quietly, studying some of the documents his group had found while Pandie ran between others commenting in a loud voice about how scared he had been.

Macleod approached Peter McKinney. "Hi there, I'm Seoras. I think I got off to a bad start with your partner earlier. Sorry about that but sometimes the job dominates you. How have you found all this?"

The man looked up and Macleod swore his eyes seemed frightened. The light in the room bounced off a totally bald and seemingly polished head and he looked at Macleod as if he was the strangest person he had ever seen.

"It's quite obvious. We have to go down to the shore. All the evidence points to the shore. Don't you think, Seoras?"

Macleod had not given the mystery any thought, thinking it quite puerile when he had real murders to deal with. But he did not want to appear a grump and so nodded his head while Peter showed him the important detail in his deductions.

"Down to the beach, Peter. Seems a good conclusion to me." With that Macleod turned away and found Hope. "Looks like we are heading for the beach. It's freezing out there. And the storm's getting worse. Macaulay's a nutter, Hope."

"Are you not having fun?" she asked. "I'm having a hoot, and with a stunning rugby player following me, too. I can't knock this little shindig."

"Just mind," said Macleod, "his girlfriend has cast a few eyes at you already."

"And Miss Baxter at you. She might be out of the action but she's kept her eyes on you. You must be a heck of a shoulder to cry on." Hope sipped her whisky and asked Macleod if he wanted another drink.

"My coffee's fine. Watch out for Mr Johnston, total arse. Arrogant as anything."

"Well matched to his wife then," said Hope. "Oh, hang on, your watcher's about to get it on."

Lorraine Baxter had got to her feet, rather unsteadily, and had grabbed her father's jacket, pulling herself up to his ear. Macleod could not hear what was being said but faces were contorted and angry. Then Macaulay pushed his daughter to a chair and poured her another dram for her to sup. She swayed unsteadily on the chair and then seemed to settle.

"Well, everyone," announced Macaulay suddenly, "having consulted with you all, I think it's clear our visitors are coming from the beach area and may have set up home there. After dinner we shall make our way down there. You'll need to wrap up warm and we'll prep ourselves for an encounter. It's time we started getting to the bottom of this horror that's been visited on my home!"

There was a cheer from some of the participants but Macleod was watching Lorraine Baxter, who now stood on her feet.

"The beach? Out there to the beach? Are you bloody insane? Everyone, this is my dad and he's a right bastard."

Macaulay went to grab his daughter by the arm but she pushed him violently away.

"Don't try and shut me up. That man," she said, pointing at him, "that excuse of a man knows I hate blood, knows I hate all of this shit he's putting us through, but he still makes sure I come and do this. He loves it, to scare the living shit out of his girl. It's a form of chil . . ."

And she fell over. Macleod watched who reacted first and noted it was Hope and Aldo Brace who arrived at her side and began to check her over. Within a minute, they had her in an armchair, and the room was strangely quiet, although no one was missing the view.

"Well," said Macaulay, "too much to drink. She never was the best with drink. But regardless, after dinner we shall look to eradicate our foes. So now to dinner, ladies and gentlemen, sustenance for otherworldly explorers."

As others moved to the dining room, Macleod strode over to Hope and Aldo. "She okay?"

"I think so, Seoras. Just a bump but she's pissed as a newt. I think we should accompany her closely at dinner."

"Agreed," said Aldo and he called for Zara to join him. "If she sits between Zara and Hope, then she won't make a fool of herself with any of the men."

"Good idea," said Macleod.

"What he means by that," said Hope, "is that he doesn't have to babysit."

Macleod did not argue and Miss Baxter was led to dinner, propped up throughout, and then taken to find her large coat when everyone looked to dress for their night expedition to the beach. They assembled in the library where a number of lanterns were dished out to the would-be investigators. Macleod had wrapped himself in a large cloak over the outfit he was already wearing. Hope had a smart coat but it didn't look warm enough to Macleod. *But then younger people don't feel the cold like we do*, he thought.

Everyone was suitably geared up and the party gathered at the entrance hall. Miss Baxter was propped between Hope and Aldo with Zara in close formation, allegedly to catch Lorraine if she fell. *More like keeping tabs on her man.*

The wind was howling and the snow was still falling. Stepping out into a blizzard seemed foolish but Macaulay assured the party they were travelling less than a half kilometre.

Macleod stepped out into the wild force and immediately felt his face going cold. He looked ahead at the footprints of Macaulay, and tried to keep up. The party was slightly broken by the time they had crossed the lawn of the house, stepped down onto the beach and then sheltered to gather their bearings.

"The cave is up ahead," shouted Macaulay. "Just up ahead. I have never dared to go in. But they must be in there."

"Look," shouted Miss Blayney, "what the hell is that?"

In the distance was an indistinct figure near the cave Macaulay had spoken about. It seemed to have some sort of webbing at places on its body but the driving snow made it hard to see.

"After it," shouted Macaulay, "that's one of them. He's going into the cave. Pandie, you're quick, get after it, lad."

As he stepped forward to run, Pandie's hand was grabbed by Peter McKinney and the pair ran off, Peter taking a slight lead. Hope was with Miss Baxter, so Seoras decided to keep up with the front group's pace.

As he approached the cave entrance, the two partners ahead of him had already gone in. There was indeed a cave and Macleod stepped inside with his lantern. Shadows danced across the walls as he entered and he decided to watch his step as he could not see fully. As he tried to look around, Pandie and Peter returned.

"Do we wait for the others?" asked Pandie.

"That could be a while given how slow Mr Johnston is moving," said Macleod, "but maybe it's best given that we are all in this together." Macleod realised this was a rather cheesy statement but at least it made him feel like he was contributing to the whole vibe of the role-play.

"Look, I doubt they'll be that long," said Peter. "I can see Macaulay and Aldo. The American's got Johnston on his shoulders. He really is a rugby player."

"Heck of a figure," said Pandie, causing Macleod to raise his eyebrows. "Well, you to yours and me to mine."

"Indeed," said Macleod, feeling rebuked. He really did struggle with open shows of that nature. Maybe he was a bit homophobic despite his efforts to stay out of the way. *It must just be in me, but I need to knock it out. Modern age and all that.* But Macleod wasn't sure he believed it.

Macaulay approached and shouted at the small forward group. "What are you hanging about for, let's see what's there? You haven't been in already, have you?"

"Just inside," said Pandie. "Peter insisted I was not enough holding his hand, wanted the rest of you as well."

"Come on," shouted Johnston. "It's damn cold outside in this wind; let's get inside. Get up that cave, McKinney. Go on!"

Peter looked at Pandie and got a look of annoyance from his partner. "Do I have to go, then?" asked Pandie. Peter shook his head and ran off into the cave taking a lantern with him. Macleod followed with Pandie but they could not match the pace of the man ahead.

The light displayed from the lantern was reasonable but the area of the floor was not well lit if the lantern was held up by the face and as Macleod held his, Pandie looked into the distance where the hint of another light was shining ahead. Macleod was not running but striding, having controlled his walking like a good beat officer did. It had been years but the rhythm never left you.

And then Pandie fell over. There was a loud yell and Macleod reached down to grab the man's arm. He had gone chin first into the floor and there was a large cut under his chin which was dripping blood.

"Here," said Macleod, giving the man a handkerchief for his chin.

"God that floor came up quick. Jesus, that stings."

Macleod decided to ignore the blasphemy and checked the man's eyes to make sure he was cogent and steady. "You don't look that bad."

"Always nice to get a compliment from a man in uniform," said Pandie and flashed a cheeky smile. Macleod was not sure how he felt at this but now was not the time for any debates on his attitudes.

"Pandie, was that you?" shouted a voice from up ahead.

"Yeah, can't see my own feet. You keep going, I'm coming. The good detective is sorting me out."

"Okay, there's some symbols and stuff up here I'm going to check out. It looks a bit like . . ."

There was a loud crash and a cry which reverberated around the cave. From behind came a call.

"What the hell's that?"

Macleod did not wait for Pandie to recognise that something was wrong and he ran off deeper into the cave. From the walls, he was assaulted by paintings and carvings indicating tentacles and strange shaped people and creatures. But he ignored this sideshow, keen to make sure that Peter was alright.

He nearly started as his light shone on a large device that was tight to the wall. It was of a metal construction and seemed to have a pivot point, which then allowed an elongated rectangle to swing round and sweep everything into the wall. Macleod swung his light up to where it had crashed into the wall and saw a squashed figure. But it was white, a skeleton.

He breathed a sigh of relief but then something caught his eye further down. It was a dark patch and he touched it with his fingers bringing it to his nose first and then to his lips. It was blood, not pig's blood, but if he was sure of anything, this was human. Blood from a skeleton did not make sense, so he began to look closer with his lantern.

Of course, just because it was human blood did not mean Macaulay had not set this up. Who knew how far the man would go with this charade. He grabbed the mechanism as he heard footsteps behind him.

"What's that?" laughed Pandie. "Bloody hell, he's really going to town with this crap, isn't he?"

Macleod nodded but then he managed to pull the mechanism back slightly. There was something behind the skeleton. A head fell to one side and looked at him with no recognition. Peter McKinney was now even more silent than he had been over the last day and would speak no more.

"Where's Peter gone?" asked Pandie, and Macleod turned around to see a happy enquiring face. As the poor light showed Macleod's face, he saw Pandie's' expression change from one of fun to that of desperate incomprehension.

"Back," said Macleod, "taking the man's shoulders with each hand and gently pushing him away from the mechanism. "Don't come closer, back."

"Peter? Is Peter in there?"

"Back, walk back, please just walk back."

"Peter! Peter! How?"

"McGrath! McGrath, I need your help, Detective."

Macleod held Pandie as he collapsed on his shoulder, his body convulsing, shaking.

"No! No! Let me see him!"

Footsteps came around the corner in the cave. "Sir?"

"Take Mr McKinney and keep everyone back. There's been a terrible accident."

"Sir?" asked Hope.

"At least I think it's an accident."

Chapter 08

"That's it—all closed off, McGrath. Baltic out there. And the wind's really kicked in. I doubt they've seen snow like this up here in a long while."

Macleod was shaking the snow off his long period overcoat as he stood in the front entrance. Beside him, Aldo Brace was carrying out the same procedure along with Anders Karlsen. Unlike Mr Brace, Karlsen was becoming a physical wreck.

"He was just hung there. His eyes so bleak, so gone."

"No talking like that once we go in please, Mr Karlsen. There's a man in there who's just lost his partner and he doesn't need any other reminders from us. Mr Brace, no discussion of what you've just seen either, please. Many thanks for your assistance, gentlemen." Macleod took Hope to one side and whispered in her ear. "Anything from this end."

"It's all very quiet as you would expect but something's brewing. They've all been in shock to some degree, but Lorraine Baxter has the evil eye for her father. Miss Blayney has been rather inquisitive for some reason, asking everyone, except me, what had happened. And Zara Dawson's a bit close to crumbling. The Johnstons are fine though. And the housekeeper and her son have been good. Everyone's had a stiff drink and there's some tea and scones coming."

"Good, Hope. I need to contact the relevant people. I'm suspecting this might not be easy, given the weather."

"I've already spoken to the housekeeper. She sent her son up the road and it's totally blocked." Hope raised her shoulders. "Also, the phone lines are down as is the mobile signal. They haven't got a radio in here but there's one in a boat down by the harbour. You'd have to go back out."

"It can wait until the morning. There's nothing anyone's going to do now. Get back in, Hope, and make sure they all stay calm and we'll get everyone to bed soon. Someone might need to keep a watch on Pandie though. If he heads out to the cave tonight, he'll freeze."

Hope made for the door through to the corridor for the library and Aldo Brace intercepted her. He had shaken off his now-covered jacket and was looking immaculately attired.

"Your Inspector is very impressive. Very calm in a crisis, like yourself. You're taking this all in your stride."

"It is my job, Mr Brace."

"I know what's happened is horrible but do we need to become formal. Call me Aldo, please. You seem to almost thrive in the circumstances."

Hope smiled. She recognised a come-on when she heard one. "Isn't Miss Dawson a more suitable match for you?"

The man seemed stunned by Hope's directness but he recovered well. "Zara is still a child, something I have realised rather late. It's good for publicity as my agent says but sometimes I want a real woman to talk to."

"Just to talk to," laughed Hope. "But I know what you mean. Sometimes I need the touch of a good man or woman."

There was a sudden drop in Aldo's features before he recovered and smiled. However, Hope did not miss that kind of response and was not surprised when the man walked on ahead entering the room first, almost leaving her for dead.

Arsehole, there's a lot of men would have enjoyed that comment. I haven't been with a girl in years. Actually, just the once. It's funny what effect it has on people.

Hope entered the library and found Lorraine Baxter standing in front of her father, lambasting him for recent events.

"Every time you have to be gross, you have to make it gory and ugly and whatever sort of shit normal people don't engage in. And this is the result. You killed a man. You bloody killed a man."

Pandie was wailing in his chair with Miss Blayney trying to comfort him. Zara Dawson was also in tears. Hope heard the door open behind her and a voice whispered in her ear.

"Everyone's fine then, holding it together well. Good job, Detective."

As Macleod walked past Hope, she gave him a swift gentle punch in the side. He did not look back, instead walking to the centre of the room and standing on a small table. Clapping his hands, he scanned the room so he could see that everyone was looking at him.

"McGrath, can you get the staff in too, for this?"

There was a minute's delay until Mrs Smith and her son, Kyle, entered the room. Then with another quick scan, Macleod began.

"Everyone, I realise that many of you are quite distressed at recent events. Before I begin, let me offer Mr McKinney our most sincere condolences. I barely knew your partner but he seemed a decent man and was obviously loved by you.

"Normally in this situation, I would have contacted the local Police and they would be here to take over. However, the

71

weather seems to have thwarted any actions I can take. The telephone lines and the mobile masts are down. The road is impassable and to be outside tonight would amount to foolishness. Thus, we are all staying here. Given the previous forecast, that may even mean a few days. Please try to stay calm and co-operate with each other to make this delay as peaceful as possible.

"Now I believe there is food coming and I suggest as the hour is now almost nine that we eat and then retire to our rooms. In the morning I may need to recruit some of you for my investigations into what exactly happened. Until then, don't wander, stay to your rooms and the library and dining rooms. Other mechanisms could be faulty. I assume these rooms are safe, Mr Macaulay?"

"Yes, yes. Nothing in these rooms." Macaulay was still white as a sheet and trembling. His daughter glowered at him, and an accusing finger was still pointed. She was not letting up even though she was having to be quiet.

"Good. So please eat, drink. Tea, or a whisky, but keep it sensible, I don't want to have to deal with any drunken shenanigans in the circumstances. There's enough on our plate. Thank you, and again, Mr McKinney, I'm deeply sorry for your loss."

As Macleod stepped down, Johnston took him to one side. "Once you've solved the problem, I assume we can continue the weekend?"

Macleod felt like he'd been hit by a truck from the wrong side of the motorway. He just did not see that question coming. "No! Are you insane? There's been a death. We shall ride out the storm, get the experts in, and send everyone home. Have some compassion; a man's partner has died."

When Johnston went to say more, Macleod held his hand to his face and made his way to Pandie McKinney. The man was still crying, a large whisky in his hand.

"I'm deeply sorry, Pandie. I can't imagine losing a partner." This was a lie, of course, but this was not about him.

"Husband, Inspector, he was my husband."

"Forgive me. It's a different world and I struggle to say the right things at times. Of course, sir, your husband. I'll do my best to find out why it happened."

Pandie nodded and then looked up suddenly at Macleod. "We thought it would be me. With my activism on equal rights. I've had threats before but never Peter. I wasn't expecting him to leave first."

Macleod went to ask more but the man broke down again and Macleod banked the question for another time. Beside Pandie, Melanie Blayney knelt on the floor and held the man's hand.

"Can I ask you something, Miss Blayney?"

"Of course, Inspector."

Macleod watched the woman stand. She was still in her costume which, given what had happened, seemed inappropriate—dressed like a woman out to attract. Her figure was hard to ignore but Macleod was resolute.

"Stay with Mr McKinney, please. He needs a gentle touch right now and you seem to have it."

"Of course," said the woman, and smiled. "You can count on me."

Macleod watched the gleam of the teeth and then the knowing wink. It hardly seemed the occasion but Miss Blayney was looking to impress. Something was wrong though. She did not seem to be showing off because she liked the limelight;

73

there was something forced about it. He did not know what he was feeling in his gut but there was something disturbing his senses. If he could only put a finger on it.

The food arrived and Macleod eagerly tucked into scones and coffee. His time at the cave had left him chilled inside and this was beginning to turn him around. Given the weather there was nothing else he could really do tonight. The scene of the accident was covered up as best he could. He had taken as many photographs as he could with his mobile. He had sent for it almost immediately and then realised on its arrival that there was no signal. Try as he might there was no signal anywhere. And then the telephone lines were down.

Kyle Smith, the chef, said that the only mobile mast that reached here came from a little further south and that all others were masked. And so annoyed as he was that he had not got the investigation going, or at least reported, Macleod tried to settle himself into a calm mind to deal with a lot of upset people. In truth, some were more upset than others. And as he watched them from the comfort of an armchair, he noted some details. Aldo Brace seemed to be coping well with the tragedy unlike his partner, Zara Dawson who was simply falling apart. Not that Aldo seemed to care. He was hovering around Hope but not talking to her. Then he would gravitate to Johnston and pass a few words.

Macaulay and his daughter were still at loggerheads although they were keeping their conversation quieter in respect of Pandie, or at least that was the reason Macleod put on it. Christine Johnston was having a hard time as Anders Karlsen, ignored totally by Lorraine Baxter, was gibbering to the older woman. Macleod could see the signs of shock and panic, but at least he was talking to someone impassive, not reactionary.

The staff were coping admirably well. Polite as always, Mrs Smith gave a no nonsense attitude and even chastised the odd guest if their tone became too down or flippant.

But inside Macleod was bothered. There was a real mix of shock and ambivalence. If the whole party had gone into some sort of quiet state of respect, or even of panic, he would have been more than content. But they were so mixed. And Melanie Blayney was still shooting eyes at him. *Well, some women liked power but she could do a lot better,* he joked to himself.

Hope came over and knelt in front of him. Leaning forward in his seat, Macleod offered to get up and let her sit down.

"It's fine, sir, though I appreciate the thought. I think it's about time to get everyone up to bed. There's talk starting and none of it healthy, asking if it wasn't an accident, how would people know?—the usual crap we get. But everyone's on edge and this is a confined place, nowhere to send the agitated away to so I think you should announce bedtime."

"You make me sound like nanny." He watched Hope raise her eyes. "Stop it. Right there." He leaned over closer. "Something feels wrong, I can't say what but there's a bad feeling in my gut. I don't think we should be in separate rooms tonight."

Hope nearly burst out laughing. "That's a pretty corny come-on."

"I'm serious. I'll sleep in the chair but I can't say what but there's something wrong here. I haven't been this good at my job without listening to my gut."

"You think there's foul play? You're not just getting carried away with all the costumes and that."

Macleod raised his eyebrows now. "Trust me. And bring pyjamas. And a dressing gown. As thick and woolly one as you can that covers you from head to foot."

Hope grinned but she nodded her ascent. It was not that Macleod felt a fool for putting these plans forward but he knew if the station ever found out there would be hell to pay. Yet the feeling inside was so strong that he did not hesitate with his action.

"Okay, everyone, I think it is time to retire. Best thing for everyone is to get a good night's sleep and we'll see what the weather brings in the morning. I intend to investigate the mechanism tomorrow with Mr Macaulay's assistance and hopefully be able to send most of you on your way home. Until then, I request that you stay calm and keep to your room until morning. Mrs Smith," said Macleod to the housekeeper, "kindly lock up in an hour's time. That should give everyone enough time to get to bed. No more alcohol, please."

Hope advised she would go upstairs and move her things to his room and took the room key from Macleod. He sat on the chair before the now dying fire and began to think through permutations in his head. *What if it wasn't an accident? Who would do it? Who could do it? How was the mechanism controlled? Macaulay had said it was remotely operated but that this trap had been set so that it was to go off before the investigator arrived. All they would see was a fake body being slammed against the wall. It should not have gone off early. The setting had been programmed and no one had been in the control room that only Macaulay had a key to. He would go through that in the morning.*

The wind howled around the house as he climbed the stairs, everyone else in bed except for Mrs Smith, who was locking up. As he rounded the top of the flight onto his floor, he saw Aldo Brace entering a room at the end of the floor. It was not the one he remembered Aldo being in and then he saw Mrs Johnston's head appear briefly. Macleod had halted in the dim landing and believed she had not seen him.

On entering his room, he saw Hope in her pyjamas stretching out in a yoga pose. It was stunning view of her behind so he turned away and began fumbling in his sock drawer for no reason at all.

"Sorry, sir. Just getting my yoga in before bed. You should try it sometime. I'll give you a lesson sometime."

"No," said Macleod, a little too quickly, "very kind but no. Not my thing."

"Very freeing, sir, especially if you strip down for it. Nothing better to wind away . . ."

"No!" blurted Macleod. He had gotten Hope into a place in his mind where he could admire her and not feel like he was gawking at her—simply enjoy her presence and her wit. He was not going back to the place where she occupied more physical thoughts. "Thank you but no. I'm ready to sleep. Think I'll just wear these."

Macleod sat in the seat and stretched out, letting himself relax. Hope went to the bed and brought a large rug over to him. She tucked it around him and then bid him goodnight.

"Now who's being nanny?" he asked.

He watched her laugh and skip over to the large bed, throwing the covers up and then snuggling under them. An arm then snaked out and turned off the light. Macleod struggled to get to sleep and sat thinking about what Jane was up to. It kept thoughts of the case and his partner asleep in his room at bay until he fell into a deep slumber.

Chapter 09

Hope was standing with one arm thrust out in front of her, cross in her hand. The dark-haired man before her had fangs dripping blood but also a bare, masculine chest that would not look amiss at a stripper's recital. Horrified by this beast, yet strangely allured by him too, she threw off her glasses and shook out her hair. The wind roared through the cemetery and Hope became aware of other creatures bursting forth from the graves around her. Some had maggots crawling from them; others seemed scantily clad and whilst having soil dropping from their shoulders, still looked like they belonged in a top-shelf magazine.

"Hope Van Helsing, only you could have escaped from my daughter's clutches." The man stepped forward, chest bared to the wind, like there was a long speech coming. "Only you could have stuffed the raw garlic in their throats as they enjoyed your perfection. But you will not best me. I shall slay you and drink your blood before taking you to heights no undead has ever reached. You shall be my bride, my lover, my all."

"Not today, Count," Hope cried and from nowhere she drew a sword, swirling it as his eyes gazed at her. She stared back and spun the sword around her wrist in an impossible fashion before turning and swing the weapon in a long arc, decapitating the count. As the rest of the creatures howled, Hope ran amok, dispatching them to the corners of the graveyard, or maybe to hell itself.

"Good," said a figure from the corner of the cemetery. "You have learned well, my child; one day you shall be as great as I—you shall be the scourge of hell itself."

Turning around, her sword dripping blood and catching a ghoul with a casual punch, Hope saw Macleod standing in a billowing cape, an immaculate suit beneath and a wide-brimmed hat on his head.

Hope opened her eyes. Above her was the panelled ceiling and she remembered she was in the house on the Isle of Harris. Slowly she lifted her head and saw Macleod sitting in the chair, where he had said he was going to sleep the night. And she was in his bed, covers pushed back.

What the hell was that? Dracula, or a stud Dracula? And Macleod! My child? Seriously, that's creepy.

Macleod had not changed his clothing but was obviously awake listening for something.

"Hey, when you said you'd take the chair I thought you were at least going to sleep." She saw Macleod look over and then reach for his woollen jumper. He threw it at her and she caught it but she hadn't missed his initial stare. *Oops! I guess the girls would have been a bit obvious. Still, he said to stay in here, his problem.*

"Put that on; it's cold," said Macleod.

Fair enough, she thought and hauled it on. "Sorry. I should have kept the covers up. But it was you who invited me to bed."

Hope watched him turn away without comment and make for the door. As she climbed out of the bed, he seemed to be

79

listening to something outside. Or maybe he was being polite, in case she exposed anything else. She chuckled to herself. It was a different day now. She didn't mind him looking and he'd thankfully never said anything inappropriate. And he was a decent boss. This gut feeling he had must really be bothering him though.

"What's up?" asked Hope

"Someone moving," said Macleod. "Opened the door to the balcony."

"Is that what that bloody draft is? Some people don't give a shit about others." Hope saw his attempt to hide his disgust at her use of the S-word. *It's everyday language now.*

Then someone screamed.

She saw Macleod open the door and scan the hallway. Hope raced up behind him and looked over his shoulder. There was no one about the ornate landing but a door was open to an exterior balcony and the wind blew hard down the opening between bedrooms. Hope caught her breath as the wind passed across her pyjama bottoms.

She watched Macleod take off to the balcony and then race along it, looking over the edge. There were voices now coming onto the landing as she followed her boss to the balcony, her bare feet screaming at her that they did not want to step out into the cold. As she reached him, she looked over his shoulders and saw a figure below, hunched over a set of spikes beneath, two spikes having gone right through him.

"Bloody hell, Seoras. Poor bastard. Jump?"

"I doubt it," said Macleod, as they both peered into the darkness below "Rarely do people stab themselves in the back before jumping."

"What's happened?" asked a voice at the balcony door.

"Take them back," ordered Macleod and Hope turned and instantly pushed back Zara Dawson and Aldo Brace onto the landing. She shut the door behind her.

'Stay here. No one goes outside until the DI comes back in. Hope looked back over her shoulder and saw Macleod looking around the balcony. Like someone demented, he spun round and round before shaking his head. Then he walked back to the door and joined Hope inside. He pulled her close and whispered in her ear.

"No footprints! There're no footprints. It doesn't make any sense. Dagger in his back and no footprints."

Hope stared at Macleod disbelievingly. "Are you sure?"

"Has someone been injured?" asked Aldo Brace. "Did someone jump? I'll go down and take a look. I'm a first aider—seen a few injuries in the rugby, too."

"No!" shouted Macleod. "Everyone stay here and gather over at that wall. I want a roll check now." Again he grabbed Hope's shoulder. "Get downstairs and make sure he's dead. And keep anyone else away."

Hope nodded and started to run down the stairs. She realised she did not have any shoes on and thought about returning but if someone else got there first they could change the scene. Macleod's intuition had been right.

On reaching the bottom of the stairs, Hope raced to find a door, only to see that it was locked. She grabbed a large sword from the wall and prepared to bring it down on the lock. Then from the corner of her eye she saw the row of keys. The housekeeper had indeed locked up but she had left the keys beside the rear door. Macleod would not be happy but then again, the woman had only thought there had been an accident. Why would you hide the keys?

Opening the door, Hope grimaced as her feet stepped into the cold snow. The ground was easy to run over but she was fighting hard to stop the cold flowing up her legs. The pyjama bottoms provided little protection from the wind and in truth the woollen jumper was not preventing her from being chilled to the core.

As she reached the man pierced by the railings, she saw his face, eyes closed and his body slumped. She slapped the face and got no response. She tried for a pulse and again there was nothing. He was dead. Slowly lifting the head, she saw the face of Macaulay. His bright blue pyjamas were stained a deep red in the dark.

From behind she heard footsteps and then a voice asking, "Who is it?"

Hope recognised Lorraine Baxter's tone immediately. "Back, back away, now! You need to back away." The look of recognition tore across Miss Baxter's face and she started running forward towards the corpse. Hope intercepted her and wrapped her arms around the woman before gently pushing her away.

"No! No! It can't be! No!"

"Back, back inside we go," said Hope forcefully but with sympathy.

"I told him I hated him. I told him I wished him dead with his bloody games. Shit! No!"

The woman's body jerked as Hope held her and the legs suddenly went leaving Hope carrying her weight. Her own feet now going numb, Hope struggled to carry the woman who was only in a simple dressing gown.

"Sir! I need help. Lorraine Baxter's collapsed. Do we have a medic amongst them?"

"Get inside! We're coming," was the reply. Hope dragged the woman through the open door and into the corridor leading to the rear of the house. She laid her down, hopefully into a recovery position shape. The basic first aid training was always something Hope did not like but it was serving her well now. But as she stood shivering in the corridor, Hope thought back to the body she had seen. Macleod had been right. There was a dagger in the back. She had not had time to reach for it, or to take a proper look but the shape was there in her mind. Macaulay was murdered, surely. This changed everything.

The housekeeper, Mrs Smith came running up to Hope and immediately knelt down to Miss Baxter. Seeing her injured party being attended to, Hope sat down on a bench in the corridor as others arrived. Macleod was ordering them to stay back and then looked towards Hope.

"Is she okay?"

"Just fainted, sir, I think. It's not a good sight."

"Okay," said Macleod. "Are you okay?"

"Just bloody cold. Otherwise fine. And sir?" Hope indicated for Macleod to lean over so she could whisper. "It's Macaulay and he was murdered. You were right—knife in the back."

Hope watched Macleod look around him, aware like her that there was a murderer among them. Watching his face, she saw him chewing over his options but surely, he knew like her, they were on their own, just the pair of them. She watched his eyes roam the suspects and the casualty on the floor and she knew he was working out how to contain this.

"Right, everyone! I want everyone to go to the library at this time. Mr Smith, help your mother by getting a fire lit and then I want a hot drink all round. McGrath, help Mrs Smith, get Miss Baxter to the library and then come back here."

Hope nodded. She had expected as much. Contain everyone with all eyes on each other while they got a look at the crime scene. But after that? Still, it meant her moving and her feet would be glad of the action, if she could feel them.

When she had helped Mrs Smith and was assured that all the guests and the Smiths were in the library with instructions not to leave, Hope sought out her boss again. She found him taking photographs of the body.

"We'll need quite a few people to shift him," said Macleod. "Even then I reckon if we don't do it soon, he'll freeze. But I want to check the balcony again, see where that knife came from. Did someone throw it? It's not right in his back. It's off to the left-hand side somewhat."

Together they climbed the stairs and made their way back onto the balcony, Hope diverting to the room to pick up her boots and a coat. When she got onto the balcony her boss was staring at the wall behind it.

"Look Hope, he must have gone over around here, it's just after the window to the balcony ends and you have this run of solid wall until the next window to another landing. He may have been running away and looking to change landings quickly. Maybe heading for a safe spot."

Hope looked at the wall and noted the ivy that was covered in snow. Despite her extra footwear and garment, she was still cold. But as she scanned the wall she noted that there was a piece of green ivy that seemed to have shaken off the white invader that had fallen from the sky. It looked like it had literally given a little twist to free off the snow. Hope reached with her hand behind the ivy and found a gap.

"Something here, sir. I'm just going to reach inside."

"Careful. You don't know what sort of crazy nonsense is

here," said Macleod.

"Ah, shit! Sorry, sir, just a pointy bit but I've got a hold." Pulling hard, Hope drew out a long pole from the wall. At the end of it was a clasp that opened when the pole reached its full extent from the wall. When Hope let it go, the clasp closed as the pole was pulled back into the wall.

"One of his games?" queried Macleod.

"But he would have known about it. And are they not designed to miss?"

"Tell that to Peter McKinney. Something is wrong here, McGrath, and we are stuck right in it. Let's check his room before we go back to the rest of them. We need to work this out quick, Hope, because I have a hunch that this is not the last trick to go wrong."

Chapter 10

Macleod sent Hope downstairs to find out where Macaulay's room was in the house and took the opportunity to change in his room. When she came back upstairs, he offered Hope the chance to do the same, but she said she would grab a shower when they were complete for the night. *She probably wants to stay in that garb,* thought Macleod, *as she does suit it. Classy but still very alluring. She certainly knows how to work her clothing, unlike me. Look like a made-up clown when I go smart.*

Macaulay's room was at the very end of the landing their own rooms were on and Macleod cautiously opened the door. He reached in and found a light switch flicking it on. The room was bathed in a warm glow from several down lighters and Macleod stepped inside the door before turning to Hope.

"Be careful. Who knows where he's set up traps. And while they may be well-intentioned, they are almost certainly deadly."

Hope nodded and stepped past her boss in a protective fashion. Macleod watched her step around the room, checking drawers and other furniture, picking up small pieces of paper and other knick-knacks. The room was tastefully decorated in the baronial fashion and had several large paintings on the

86

wall. But where Macleod had expected to see serious looking lairds of old, there were large creatures, tentacled and with gross features.

"His family were pretty ugly," said Hope, seeing Macleod's stare.

"Who in their right mind puts this sort of stuff on their wall?"

"Part of the game, Seoras. Those are the Elder gods from the game we were playing. I take it you didn't find his presentation stimulating."

He saw Hope grin before continuing her search. But something was bothering Macleod. Everything was so neat, not a thing out of place. If he had been disturbed enough to get onto the balcony, there should be some signs. He was getting away from something. So there should be signs. There was also no sign of anything being covered up, reset from a disturbance. You could usually see subtle signs. Redressing a room was no easy task and there had not been a lot of time between Macaulay's death and everyone being out on the landing.

"Anything, Hope?"

His red-haired colleague turned around and nodded, holding a small book in her hand. "This has got notes on the mechanisms and stuff like that. Seems to be a concept design for this weekend. Might be worth a read."

"Good. Bring it. He didn't flee from here so he must have been in another room. We'll need to check them. Come on; let's get everyone up and open the rooms."

"Wait," said Hope. "Why don't we see if they are open? Take a look without them knowing."

"That's not right," said Macleod. "You know we should search with approval."

"But if they are open, then what's the harm? I can guard the stairs, or you can and the other can have a quick look."

"You know what the harm is."

"Look, sir, Seoras, if you are right and this is murder and not a couple of accidents like it looks to me, then we are stuck with a murderer among us and no way of calling a halt to everything. Who knows when we'll get to civilisation, get any back-up. Until then it's you and me and we need to be ahead of the game. It's about survival as much as catching a criminal. If your instincts are right, we need to be very smart."

Macleod looked at the pleading face before him, eyes gazing over the top of the thick, black-rimmed spectacles. There was a large degree of truth in what she said. The weather should break but it could be a day, maybe two. When would they get a chance to leave or get reinforcements in? She was right. "Okay, but open doors only. We can always be just checking on people in that case."

Hope smiled and left the room followed by Macleod. She checked the first door and opened it. Switching the light on, she gazed around while Macleod watched the top of the stairs. She was back out of the room inside a minute.

"I'd say it's Pandie's. Two sets of male clothes, some clothes thrown here and there but nothing that looks like a fight or struggle."

"Okay," said Macleod, "next one, quick!"

The door next to Pandie's opened and Hope searched again. "It's Miss Baxter's, sir," she advised on exit. "Strange though, two separate beds. Looks like Anders and her are not shagging."

"They are not intimate, Hope. The word is intimate."

"Yes sir, they are not intimately shagging."

Macleod tried to look annoyed but broke into a grin. Her

crass attitude at times was actually part of her attraction, part of her roguish character. Sure, she could refine it but it would be obvious she had capitulated from her true self.

"Just get on with it," said Macleod.

Working up the landing back to the stairs, the next room was clearly the Johnston's and was immaculate with every item hung or placed—certainly no sign of a struggle. There were then two rooms left but both seemed to be locked.

"That's annoying," said Macleod, "these rooms could probably tell us something, even if it's just that Macaulay was imagining someone after him."

"Just a moment," said Hope, and she reached inside her blouse.

"What are you doing?" asked Macleod.

"Always keep them in here, where prying hands don't reach. They're not big anyway and I can conceal them easily."

Macleod was more than a little confused but turned and focused on the stairs. He kept looking away, aware of where Hope was fumbling until he felt a tap on his shoulder. In her hands were a small set of tools he recognised.

"No! We would be breaking in."

"And I said it was survival. If you are right, it's survival. And I'm going with your gut, sir. And it's just a look."

Macleod thought hard. She was right, much as he hated the idea of breaking into a room. Survival—that was the word. He nodded and walked along to the top of the stairs, whispering behind him, "Be quick."

It was only two minutes later that he heard her exit and saw Hope walking along the landing towards him but indicating with her thumb that he needed to look. Without hesitation, they crossed and he looked into the first room. There were upturned chairs and items swept off the dressing table. One picture was torn. He saw two cases and presumed this was Aldo Brace and Zara Dawson's room.

Quickly, he entered the second room which had clothes thrown about and a bed that was disturbed, sheets everywhere. There was a single case by the wall and the en suite showed female products. Surely this was the room of Melanie Blayney.

Macleod heard a cough from Hope and quickly exited the room. There was a single set of footsteps coming up the stairs. He saw the top of Mrs Smith's head rising from below as he joined Hope.

"Detectives, sorry to disturb you but the guests are asking if they can return to their rooms. It seems some want to sleep, sir, as it is close to the early morning being almost four 'clock."

"I understand, Mrs Smith, but if you could ask them to wait a while longer and I shall be down presently to advise them further. It won't be long before they can get to bed. It's been a rough night on us all."

"Very good, sir. I shall return to them and advise them so."

Macleod watched the woman descend the stairs and gave a nod to Hope to lock the rooms back up. She returned two minutes later and looked at him, raising an eyebrow.

"Two rooms showing distress. How do you want to play it," she asked.

"Melanie Blayney. We'll talk to her first as I know she's hiding something. Did you see how she watched people? Something is not right about her, almost acts like you . . ." Macleod was about to say *or me* but he didn't get the chance.

"She's nothing like me. I don't give it up to men like that."

"I meant like a detective, Hope. Like you, *or me*, she watches, reads, and plays people. She's hiding something."

"Right," said Hope, "like a detective."

"And for what it's worth, I don't see you that way. You're no tart, even if I had a more dated sense-of-clothing protocol."

Clothing protocol, where did I get that phrase from. She always sets me on edge if I'm talking about her looks.

"I know, boss. I'll mind my clothing protocol though."

"Come on, let's go see the suspects."

They descended the stairs in silence, each thinking through what they needed to do next. Macaulay's death threw up a lot of unanswered questions but the main one staring at them was what had put him into such a state that he appeared to be running away from someone? And where was he going?

On entering the library, Macleod saw Anders Karlsen pacing the floor while the Johnstons appeared to be snoring in some armchairs. Miss Baxter looked to be drinking again—a large brandy—and was being attended to by Melanie Blayney. Zara Dawson and Aldo Brace looked like they were in a heated discussion, with a lot of finger pointing and Pandie was simply staring out of a window. The chef, Kyle Smith, was sitting with his mother, yawning.

"Thank you for your patience," said Macleod on entering the room. "Before I let you go to your beds I'd like to ask if any of you saw Mr Macaulay before he was on the balcony. Any time since we left the library for bed until his unfortunate demise."

Mrs Johnston cleared her throat. "We saw him up the stairs and into his room, Inspector. Miss Blayney can vouch for that; she was with us. But we deposited him in his room as he was not in the best of states."

"That's right," said Aldo Brace, "and we were behind—Zara and myself, we saw him being dropped off at his room."

"Anyone see him after that?" asked Macleod.

There was silence. But then Zara Dawson put up her hand.

"Yes, Miss Dawson. It's okay; it's not school. You don't have to raise your hand—just speak," said Macleod.

"Well, I heard him speaking to someone. I had gone over to see if Mr McKinney, Pandie, was all right. Can't have been easy going to an empty room. And I heard him speaking to someone."

"What was he saying?" asked Hope.

"I don't know. It was very low key."

"That was me," said Mrs Smith. "Just making sure everything was all right and what time he wanted everyone up at and the breakfast ready for."

"And what time did he say?" asked Macleod.

"For what?"

"The breakfast, Mrs Smith."

"Oh, well . . . nine." The woman shrugged her shoulders.

"And Mr McKinney, did you hear anything when Miss Dawson came over to your room?" asked Macleod.

"No, but she did come over. It was very sweet of her because I did need the company."

"Anyone else have any other sightings, I should know about?"

There was silence and Macleod felt a yawn coming on. "Okay, then. I suggest we all go up to bed and lock our rooms until morning. I realise some of you may be a little spooked but lock your door and try to sleep. I'd also suggest being in pairs."

"Why?" asked Mr Johnston. "Do you suspect some sort of foul play? I mean the man got caught out by one of his own traps. Another accident it would seem."

"Possibly, Mr Johnston, but I'd sleep easier knowing every-one was not alone. Shall we say ten o'clock for breakfast, Mrs

Smith? Mr Smith, please stay with your mother tonight."

"Shall I stay with Pandie?" asked Miss Blayney.

"That would be good," said Hope.

"Indeed," said Macleod, "but can you stop here a while with me, Miss Blayney. Everyone else please retire. McGrath, can you accompany Mr McKinney until I come upstairs with Miss Blayney."

As everyone exited the room, Anders Karlsen grabbed Macleod. "Do you think he was murdered? God's sake, I didn't sign up for this."

"What did you sign up for?" asked Macleod.

"I'm an escort," he whispered into Macleod's ear.

"Then escort your client to her room and stay with her," said Macleod. "You'll be safer there."

After everyone had left, Miss Blayney pulled an armchair close to the dying fire. Without asking, she pulled one up for Macleod as well. She sat down and crossed her legs making sure everything below the knee had escaped her dress. She leant back touching her cleavage and then stared at Macleod.

"I'm actually looking to ask some questions, Miss Blayney, not make a pass," said Macleod.

"Of course, Inspector, but no reason we can't enjoy ourselves. It's been a rough night or should I say morning?"

"Who are you?"

"I'm sorry," said Miss Blayney.

"Who are you? You're no model. Or if you are, that's a side show to your main event. Yes, you have the body but you look at people, reading them, sizing them up, and calculating. Just like myself, like McGrath. Who are you?"

"What makes you think I'm more than a model?"

"Everything I just said."

93

"So, intuition?"

"Experience," answered Macleod. "A lot of experience."

"If you must know, I'm a private investigator, so we're on the same side."

"Not necessarily."

"I'm looking into Miss Baxter for a client. The woman has a nasty streak and a line in coercion, and not the simple kind. I managed to get Macaulay interested in me and got an invite here where I knew his daughter would be. She's not easy to get close to."

"Did you see Macaulay tonight?" asked Macleod.

"Been in my room then? I'd have done that, too. Yes, I did see him but it wasn't me talking in his room. He came over after that, in fact quite soon after we retired. He needed some comfort and I offered. It was all a bit rough and ready to be honest, he was no class act."

"You had sex?"

"Yes Inspector, we had sex. And he has strange tastes in that too, I tell you, bit like his role-play game here. Got a bit of information about his darling daughter too, how she had asked for help recently in hushing someone up and how he had refused to help. Amazing what men will tell you when they are excited."

The woman was smiling and Macleod felt disgusted by her. This was not investigating, not a way to get to the truth. Male or female, using your body like that was sick. Also, unreliable. People will lie for pleasure.

"Was it something he could hold over her?"

"I'd say so. She'd asked someone to put the frighteners on a rival and it hadn't worked. Wanted Daddy to sort it out as the rival seemed to know it was her."

"So why didn't they come to us?"

"Evidence—makes it hard to get your interest if you don't have it."

"Anything else," asked Macleod, ignoring how the woman was trying to attract his gaze with her cleavage.

"No. I was hoping for more. What's wrong, Inspector? We could keep warm together, solve this thing. I'm great to work with."

"And I'm a pain in the arse; ask McGrath. Time for you to keep a watch on Mr McKinney. You're no fool, Miss Blayney, or whatever your real name is, but neither am I. Keep out of my way and let me solve this before someone else gets hurt."

"Of course, Seoras. But you really could do with a little fun."

"Time to retire, Miss Blayney."

The woman stood up and brushed up against Macleod making sure she contacted him with as much of her body as she could without actually knocking him down. He felt a hand grab his backside and she smiled in his face as she left the room.

Macleod laughed. He enjoyed a sexual woman but he found her just crass. The ulterior motive simply made the effort fall flat and he grinned, thinking how he had won. But she could be useful, an extra pair of eyes, albeit a dangerous pair. He switched off the light and left the library, the fire throwing a red glow around the panelled room.

One messed-up room accounted for. What had Mr Brace and Miss Dawson been up to?

Chapter 11

Macleod trudged up the stars, a tired figure. It was past four in the morning and he had been thinking hard with a brain that was trying to go back to sleep. Under normal circumstances he would have been able to let a night crew sort out the scene and give him the necessary information that morning as the sun rose, allowing a fresh Macleod to get on with the investigation. But that was not available here. It was Hope and himself, at least for another twenty-four hours.

She had called it survival and he was beginning to understand where she was coming from. Who was to say that they wouldn't be targets? But they were not meant to have been here. It should have been his boss. What was the connection between the two dead men? Or were they just tragic victims of inadequate engineering? Or was there a greater connection among all the guests?

Racist lines, homophobic links, cultural bias, employer wrong doings, deranged individuals. It was all a sea of thought that he was struggling through as he climbed on wearily up the stairs. As he reached the top he met Hope coming from Pandie McKinney's room.

"She's with him now, sir. I think all the guests are in their rooms—except for the staff, or at least I don't know as they are on a different level."

"Good, let's get inside ourselves," said Macleod.

Unlocking the door, he stepped aside to let Hope in. He was unsure if she found this patronising but she always went through, maybe as a nod to his civility. He guessed she must compromise too, allow him the less contentious ways he was guilty of.

"If you don't mind, I'm going to have a shower before bed, Seoras. You can take the bed this time and I'll take the chair."

Without a chance to answer due to Hope disappearing into the en suite, Macleod decided to change. He was sure he smelt and probably could do with a bath himself, but he was not barging in and could not wait for Hope to sort herself out. He quickly changed into his pyjamas and laid his dressing gown by his bed before climbing under the sheets.

Making a decision to go directly to sleep, Macleod tried to clear his mind of the question soup that had been occupying it. On hearing the shower start he began to think about Hope but realised that in her current situation that was not a good idea and then turned his thoughts to Jane. He wondered what she was doing. Four o'clock, she would be sleeping. His mind began to fill with sweet moments they had shared over the past few weeks, how she had looked and when they had touched. Soon he found himself drifting off, the rainfall of the shower reminding him of that afternoon in Glasgow when they got caught without their raincoats.

A scream split the air. It was accompanied by a crash. And then another scream.

"Seoras! Help! Help me, Seoras!"

Macleod threw back the bedsheets and was on his feet

quickly. But he was also groggy as he stumbled across the room to the en suite door. Turning the handle, he found it locked.

"God, Seoras! Help, bloody help!"

His mind tried to get into gear and he found himself staring momentarily at the handle. It had one of those locks you could undo from the outside with a screwdriver or flat edge. He had nothing on him, pocketless in his pyjamas. Gripping the small knob with the slat cut into it, he tried to turn it with his bare hands but he only succeeded in cutting the edge of his finger.

"Seoras, I'm hanging. I'm going to bloody fall. There's spikes down there."

Turning around, he scanned the room. Something flat was needed, and now. The dressing table, surely. He tore over and looked at the few items Hope and himself had on it. There was a tube of cream of Hope's, one she had brought in with her. But the narrow end seemed flimsy. Comb, there was a comb. He grabbed it. It was a simple plastic comb of his and the edge looked thin enough.

Back at the lock, he delicately placed the top end of the comb into the slat in the knob of the lock. His hands were shaking as he did so and he heard Hope scream again. After a few failed attempts due to shaking hands, Macleod placed the comb correctly and quickly turned the knob. He dropped the handle and the door opened.

The room had changed since his recent visit. The toilet with mirror above it was still close by the entrance but where the bath cum shower had been, there was a hole in the floor. There was floor remaining on his side of the room but it was narrow, less than a person wide. The single light was still hanging from a high ceiling and it lit up a naked Hope, hanging from the shower head which was barely still attached to the wall. The stainless steel pipe that ran up to the head was coming away from the rear wall as Hope squirmed desperately, her wet red hair hanging over white skin, buttocks and legs in constant motion trying to get some traction.

"Hold on," cried Macleod and edged along the wall towards the far end of the en suite.

"I can't, it's going, it's coming away, Seoras!"

With his back to the wall, Macleod quickly side-stepped his way along the wall and came alongside Hope. The distance between them was not great but he had little floor to stand on and she was struggling to have anywhere to pivot from, the shower head looking close to falling clean off the wall.

"Get your legs towards me, or else jump, Hope. I can't just reach you or we'll both topple in."

"Grab me," she yelled as she swung on the shower head, her legs now coming towards Macleod at speed. But the shower head came off the wall and although her legs were reaching the remaining floor, her body had toppled backwards. Hope threw out a hand and Macleod grabbed it. He began to tip forward and desperately swung his other hand to try and get some backwards motion.

"Pull, Seoras, bloody pull!"

Macleod bent his knees, stooping down and yanked hard on Hope's arm. She clattered into him awkwardly as she was thrust towards him and he grabbed her with his flailing arm. He felt her grab him and they stood on the edge, Macleod's back leaning into the wall, both breathing heavily.

"You go first, we can't both walk along here," said Macleod.

Hope nodded and then slipped off him. There was no embarrassment at their situation, just two scared individuals who knew they were not out of the woods yet. Carefully, Macleod followed the pale skin of Hope and they made their way out of the bathroom. In the bedroom, Macleod found Hope on her knees, breathing in fits. He dropped to his knees behind her and wrapped his arms round her shaking body.

"There were spikes down there. I was dead, Seoras, good as dead."

"But I got you. It's okay, I got you."

It was then Macleod noticed the commotion at his bedroom door, voices and a loud banging sound.

"What the hell's going on in there? Is everyone all right?"

It was Pandie's voice followed by similar shouts from Melanie Blayney. Macleod held onto Hope and called back.

"We're okay but wait. Something's happened. Gather everyone outside our door, including the housekeeper."

"What's happened?"

"I'll tell you when everyone's gathered. We need a minute here." And then to Hope in a quieter voice, Macleod said, "And we need to get you dried and into some clothes. Can you do that?"

Hope was quiet and still shivered. Macleod looked around for her pyjamas but they were in the bathroom. He thought about getting some of his clothing but he still needed a towel.

"I need to go back into the bathroom, okay, to get a towel. I'll be quick but you just stay here." When she nodded, Macleod quickly made his way back into the bathroom. He sought out a towel but his eyes lingered on the hole where the bath had been. Carefully he looked over into the drop and saw the spikes below.

Having grabbed a towel, he wrapped it around Hope. "Can you dry yourself? If not, I'll do it but that could be a little embarrassing for both of us," said Macleod. He saw a faint smile and then the face fell again. "Thank you. You saved me, Seoras, you bloody saved me. If not I'd have . . ."

"Don't think about it; just do for now. Dry yourself and I'll find clothes."

Outside the door of the room were murmurs and chatter and then came another knock on the door.

"Hold up. We'll be another minute," said Macleod, who quickly glanced at Hope to see how she was progressing. When he saw her standing upright drying herself, he turned his back again. Recovering the trousers she had been wearing, he also found her underwear and blouse. He grabbed his woollen jumper she had on earlier and gently laid them on the bed before telling her over his shoulder where they were and for her to tell him when she was decent.

As he stood looking at the wall, Macleod tried to think through what to do now. He had thought that sending everyone to rooms and generally containing them there, would be a way of keeping everyone safe. *Well, I got that wrong.* It was time for a new plan, but what?

"Hey."

It was Hope's voice and he turned around to see her standing there dressed. She walked up to him and took his head in her hands and stepped up and kissed his forehead. "Thank you," she whispered. "But I'm scared, Seoras. That was too close, it was . . ." Hope shivered as she spoke. "This is not like a case. We really are in danger."

Macleod nodded. "I thought isolation was the answer but now I think we may need to keep everyone together. Down in the library, that seemed to be Macaulay's safe space earlier; it's where he returned everyone to."

"Good idea. I don't want to stay in this room, not with what happened in there." She pointed to the bathroom before turning away from it.

"Okay, open the door then and let the others in. But keep them up by the bed."

Hope unlocked the door and the other guests filed in followed by Mrs Smith and her son. Johnston stepped to the front of the group. "So what the hell's been happening then, Macleod? That was a hell of a racket and screams, too."

Macleod nodded. "DC McGrath was taking a shower in the en suite. Then the bath gave way, leaving a room of spikes below. Luckily, she hung onto the shower head until I could help her get to safety. But it was close. Another accident that could have been deadly."

"Are you sure, Inspector?" asked Miss Baxter, "Dad would have put in false spikes. He was no killer."

"Come with me then," said Macleod, "but carefully. And bring that bowl of fruit, Mr McKinney."

Scared as some of the guests were, they all followed except for Hope who sat on the bed. Once everyone had a view into the en suite, Macleod took a few items of fruit and dropped them into the hole where the bath had stood. He watched as each piece of fruit that touched a spike sliced cleanly.

"Your father may have been a prankster and a weekend party mastermind, Miss Baxter, but someone has made this prank deadly. Kindly all step back into the bedroom and we'll work out what we are to do."

There was a general murmur of shock and panic but Macleod ushered the entire party through except for Anders Larsen, who was staring into the hole. Macleod took the man by the arm and led him back into the bedroom before shutting the door.

Macleod joined Hope by the bed and ran a hand across her brow. She was still chilled, whether it was shock or the room, he was not sure but he was worried for her. He had to make plans and so he turned to the rest of the group and raised his hands for quiet.

"We obviously have a situation and I'm sure you all have a lot of questions, about each other and about the house and whatever this nightmare is we are caught in. The weather outside is preventing us simply leaving, which I think we should do when we can. Until then, I suggest that we all camp out in the library and Mrs Smith can bring in what food there is and we'll build a fire. Telephones and mobiles are out so we may have to walk out."

"There's a boat, along from the harbour, sir." It was chef. "I use it to catch some of the food but it would get us away and we could get to another small harbour and maybe the roads will be better. It also has a radio. You could call the coastguard."

Macleod nodded. "Thank you, Mr Smith."

"Why are we waiting until morning? To hell with the storm we need to go before someone else is butchered," shouted Anders. "McKinney's dead, so's Macaulay; I don't want to be next, just waiting in a room for it to happen. This house is not safe."

"And outside is not safe either," said Johnston. "I'll not get anywhere. Our chef is right, let's get a small party out to the boat in the morning and they can send a helicopter for us."

A commotion broke out between the two men and Anders started cursing Johnston. Johnston rabbited on, his nose to the air and then chatter began amongst everyone else. Macleod was losing control of the situation.

"Shut it!" Hope was standing on the bed and had her hands on her hips. The sheer volume of her voice silenced everyone. "The Inspector said we go to the library. When morning comes, people can take their chances if they want with whatever. But for now, we need to set up camp and wait for morning, so haul your backsides down to the library with whatever nonsense you want from your rooms. But enough of the arguments and discussion. I want you where I can see you all. So get going."

Macleod was taken aback by Hope's directness. Her face was angry and she was defying anyone to challenge her. But then he caught her eye.

"If that's okay by you, sir."

"Good plan, Detective Constable McGrath. You heard her, ladies and gentlemen, kindly follow her instructions."

As everyone left, Macleod grabbed Hope by the arm and pulled her close. "You okay?"

Hope nodded. "I don't trust any of them. Down there we can take turns sleeping and make sure no one gets up to anything."

"The plan's good, Hope, but maybe less dramatics."

"Yes, sir. But one of those bastards tried to kill me. And they have killed two others, so I ain't taking any risks."

"Good," nodded Macleod, "but remember, we work together and we think this through. We're still the authority here."

"That's easy for you to say, sir, you weren't hanging naked above a set of spikes!"

Chapter 12

Macleod sat in a large armchair by the blazing fire in the library. As Hope had instructed, everyone was in the room, most sleeping in an array of bedding formed from mattresses, armchairs placed together, tables, and simple floor space. The room was not cold thanks to the heat generated by the log fire.

Hope was lying on a mattress beside Macleod and she was snoring lightly. In all the ways he had viewed his colleague, and some had maybe not been that helpful to his previous loneliness, he had never pictured her snoring. A woman looking that good should never snore—it was not something he had even considered. It was only in Hollywood comedies that attractive women snored, never in times of trouble or suspense.

As he looked around the room whilst drinking an enormous cup of black coffee, Macleod saw only one other person obviously awake. Anders Karlsen, the strapping blond-haired young stud was not handling the situation well. Several times he had told Macleod he was going to make a run for it and Macleod had told him to sit back down. If the man disappeared out into that storm, there was no way Macleod was going after him. If anything, the storm was getting worse.

As he stayed awake for his turn at keeping watch, Macleod let his mind wander over the situation. There were two people dead, whether by accident or deliberate murder. He'd also nearly lost his colleague. In his mind was a debate that raged between simply surviving, as Hope said, and actually solving this situation, his natural instinct.

The dead men, that was the place to start. Peter McKinney had seemed a quiet soul and rather a strange target, if it was murder. Yes, he was homosexual and that was always a possible motive from an intolerant suspect but no one had shown such prejudice. His partner, Pandie, was surely a better target, a vocal man when it came to LGBT issues. Of course, it needed to be asked: just who had actually been the target?

Macaulay's death was more awkward. He had built this whole system of elaborate traps and fictional horror scenes. But he had said it was all just a role-play horror scenario. It was extreme, but nothing said it was designed by him for murder. And he had died which is not the traditional way murderers work. They tend to see themselves as surviving to the end. But his death did mean that Macleod did not know where the control room was for the horror show. Where were the devices controlled from? How did they operate? And were they simply set wrong and it was an accident, or was there a malevolent force at work?

He didn't know and he was tired. He was also uncomfortable at the fact he had two dead bodies still in situ where they had died. Time, weather, and lack of numbers meant he was reticent to lift the men down but he was also unhappy to have to make such a decision, even if Hope backed him. In the morning someone would strike out for the boat and the radio but with everything that had gone on so far, he was not banking on a quick resolution.

At six o'clock, he woke Hope and managed to get two hours sleep. When he awoke, many people were on the move, feeding themselves from some cold meats and cereal that Mrs Smith had brought through. Macleod tried to eat as well, but his stomach was not in the mood. Outside, the dawn was just arriving and he saw the snow still coming down in a wild fashion, blown here and there by the ever-increasing wind.

"Some people are getting itchy. When are you striking out for the boat?" asked Hope.

"I'm not," said Macleod, "you are."

"Me, why me?"

"Because you are younger, fitter, and better at handling single combat than me. There's a much better chance of you handling whoever goes with you, if one of them is the killer. But I want to send at least three people and definitely two others that are not friends in any way. Don't want you out alone with two malcontents. It would be bad enough if one of them was a killer, never mind two."

"Is it Macaulay's death that has you thinking that?" whispered Hope, close in to her Inspector.

"He is the master of ceremonies and yet even after his death things have happened. I don't know if he was a player, a victim or what. But I will find out. I need to know what connects Peter McKinney, Macaulay, and our boss, or you, or maybe even me. At the moment I haven't a clue."

There was a ruckus starting across the room and Hope turned around to see what had caught her Inspector's eye. Anders Larsen was pushing Aldo Brace and the rugby player was happy to shove back.

"We need to get out of here, you idiot, before we all die. It's daylight, let's go," shouted Larsen.

"Have you seen that storm out there? You'll freeze, we'll all freeze." Aldo Brace was waving his arms at Anders, making him out to be a fool.

"And you'd keep us here. Keep us to die. Is that your plan, is it you doing this? Did you kill McKinney? Is it because he was gay? Are you some sort of American fundamentalist? God squad?"

"Enough!" bellowed Macleod. There was no way he was letting this turn into a religious matter or having people throwing accusations around that were unfounded. "I understand you are tense, Mr Larsen, but that will get us nowhere. Random accusations have no place here, so kindly keep quiet. On the issue of getting to the boat and calling for help, my DC is going to go there shortly and she needs some volunteers for the trip. Maybe yourself and Mr Brace would be so good, give us a rounded view while out there."

"Okay," said Larsen, "but if I get a chance to get to the road, I'm taking it. Understand."

"Perfectly," answered Hope, "but you'd be a fool in this weather. Stick together or you will freeze to death somewhere alone."

Macleod watched Anders Larsen's face go white at the mention of freezing to death and he thought Hope too strong in her rebuke. So, he decided he needed to get the party on the move sooner rather than later. "Okay, that's decided. I'll stay with the rest of the group but McGrath, can you organise your party? The sooner we get out of here the better for everyone."

As Hope departed the room with her party, Macleod found himself some cold breakfast, and was joined by Johnston as he looked out of the window at the snow blizzard beyond.

"Good decision, sending your deputy out there. It looks wild. And men of our age are not built for that kind of physical exertion."

Macleod wanted to punch him. *Men of our age. He jumped down a hole and nearly broke himself. I think there's a bit more left in me than you.*

"Are you feeling better? Has the leg recovered yet?" asked Macleod.

"An unfortunate incident but at least I am back to being my more-than-useful self. If you need some brain power, I am available, Inspector."

"Well, that is good to know, sir. I'll make it a point to ask for you."

Macleod ignored the man after that until Johnston retired to a chair, tired of standing on the damaged leg. He hated the idea of simply sitting around waiting for Hope to bring back some rescue news but he was also not able to run off and leave everyone unaccompanied. It was too easy for things to happen when the party was in smaller numbers.

Hope returned twenty minutes later with her party dressed in large coats and hats, prepared for the cold outside. Macleod noticed she was not wearing anything that would impede her movement and he wondered if she had enough warm clothes on. Maybe she was banking on trouble arriving.

"Get out there, get a signal to someone, and then return. And watch your back, keep them in sight at all times."

"I think these two won't be a problem. Larsen is scared witless and Aldo Brace has been checking me out, being rather friendly. You might have more issues with the remaining guests."

"Just be careful," said Macleod. "We can't be sure but I

109

reckon there's a killer here. I don't buy an erroneous setup of equipment. You said it. Survival. So watch your back, Hope."

The remaining guests walked the small party to the door to see them off. The mood was solemn and Macleod simply took it on himself to shake the hands of the men accompanying Hope. He stood at the door and watched the party move off, following initial guidance that had been provided by Kyle Smith, the chef. Macleod smiled. He was proud of his DC. She was bringing up the rear of the party letting Brace take the lead and keeping Larsen, the nervous individual, between the two calmer figures of the party. But inside he was worried for her. He was not convinced about either Brace or Larsen but he did not know why. It was not easy being a potential victim.

Macleod ushered those staying behind back into the library. Everyone was now fully awake, energy returning after a turbulent night, and Macleod wished they could all just go back to sleep. He had not had much sleep and he needed to be sharp now that Hope was elsewhere and not watching his back.

He asked Mrs Smith and her son, Kyle, to join him at the window and stood looking out until they arrived. It was a good technique to ensure that no one interrupted him. When they did, he asked them to stand and look out of the window too, ensuring no one behind them could read any of what was being said.

"I don't wish to panic anyone so please talk to the window and keep your voices low. Whilst my colleague is attempting to gain help, I thought it best that I should continue investigations and that begins with the equipment your former master was using to create this horror weekend of his. Do you know where his control room is? How we shut it down?"

Mrs Smith coughed and then stared at the snow storm. "The master had that installed on a weekend off for my son and me. At least the room anyway. He didn't want anything given away by us. It was a foreign firm that came over, Inspector. Although I made them comfortable and fed them on the initial night, they were here for over a week after that while we were on a paid holiday."

"So, you don't know where the room is?" asked Macleod.

"Not exactly," said Kyle Smith. "I know where it is roughly, which part of the house. There was an old children's nursery on the north side. You used to reach it by the stairs but when we came back it had disappeared."

"Disappeared? How do you make a room disappear?" ask Macleod.

"You build around it," said Mr Smith. "There was literally new panelling and no access. You wouldn't know it was there at all unless you had seen the previous incarnation. I can lead you to the stairs around it but I couldn't find the door. I've tried, several times, at the master's request. They did a damn good job."

"Would you have any better places to start looking, Mrs Smith?"

"No, Inspector, I'm as in the dark as my son."

"Thank you both. Not a word to the others, please. We'll start to look for this control room when my colleague returns."

Macleod remained impassive as they left, but noted that the storm was still as wild as it had been throughout the night. He looked at his watch. *How long would Hope be? Could she contact any authorities? Anyone?*

Macleod sighed, turned around, and made his way to a small table that held a flask of coffee. Pouring himself a coffee, he scanned the room. Zara Dawson and Pandie were talking at the fireside, both looking pale. The Smiths were sitting down and taking a breather. They had been working hard, keeping the guests fed and comfortable. Melanie Blayney was watching Lorraine Baxter from the corner of the room and gave Macleod a wink as she noticed his stare. Lorraine Baxter herself was a mess, eyes red from tears, and Mrs Johnston seemed to be floating around her, no doubt telling her to have a stiff upper lip. Macleod laughed inside.

And then he saw the great Mr Johnston, the man who Macleod would turn to for greater brain power. *Arrogant arse,* thought Macleod, *sitting there in a large chair, middle of the room like he's the laird. And he's actually enjoying this despite the fact people have died, others are frightened and we have a murderer on the loose. I'm not convinced about him.*

As Macleod watched, he heard a sudden deep laugh erupt in the room. He could have sworn it was Macaulay's laugh but there was a richness to the tone that suggested computer manipulation. Everyone started looking around before a yell came from the chair in the middle of the room.

"I can't get up," shouted Johnston.

Macleod started to go toward the chair but a sudden crash from the ceiling had him throwing himself to the ground. As he looked up he saw a creature with talons and small wings descend. The talons were black and covered in blood. They grabbed hold of the chair and Johnston was hauled up into the ceiling. As dust and plasterboard continued to fall, Macleod raced to the underside of the hole in the room's ceiling and looked up into another room that was devoid of any creature.

There was a crash from above and something landed out in the snow beyond the library window. Macleod raced over, looking out into the stormy scene. There was a chair lying broken in the snow but he could not see any sign of Johnston.

Chapter 13

McGrath watched the small party before her walking across the snow, deep and thick, towards the sea beyond. Through a mass of swirling white, she could see the breakers, the result of a churned-up sea that had been whipped by the wind these last few days and which showed no sign of abating. One of the options before them, at least potentially, was to take a boat for help. Looking at the waves and with no known master of the sea among them, that might be a forlorn idea.

Aldo Brace was marching ahead, but Hope had noticed one thing about him since they had first been introduced. That was his attitude and how it had changed to her. At first, when they had been on that small team with Macaulay and Mrs Johnston, he had been more than cordial, like someone who was deeply interested in her but who had a previous attachment that held him in check. But the attitude had changed sharply and she tried recalling what she had said to make it happen.

It was the quip about having a girlfriend or something like that, a statement that implied she might have more to her sexuality than just a desire to couple with men. And it had not been that strong a quip either. Whatever had happened, she was making sure she would keep an eye on him as he was a strong brute. The rugby player was well-toned and she had no idea if he knew how to fight or subdue, so she would be watching carefully.

Anders Larsen was another matter entirely. The man was a wreck at the moment and while she understood Macleod's idea of sending her out with two opposites who were unlikely to be in league with each other, he could have given her someone more useful.

The trip to the boat was said to be less than a mile by Mr Smith, the chef, and Hope was going to be only too delighted not to have to be out in this storm for long. After leaving the house, they made their way past where the helicopter had landed and onto a beach. This was going to be the easiest route according to Mr Smith as the snow looked like it had blocked up the roads and someone unfamiliar with the terrain might easily miss where the road was running.

Once on the snow-covered beach, the party walked close to where the tide was coming in as this meant a thin line of snow, the tide having removed some of the earlier falls from previous days. As the tide rolled in, the smaller crashes on the beach overwhelmed by the wind and larger breakers beyond, Hope felt a peace despite the biting cold. There was a wild beauty about this place even in the harshest of times.

Hope watched Anders Larsen stumble along, looking desperately from side to side as Aldo Brace seemed to quicken his pace. She stepped up and took Larsen by the shoulders, imploring him to hurry up. When that proved beyond him, she shouted at Brace to slow down but her calls went unheard or unheeded. Ahead, she could see the small harbour and the boat tied up to its berth but still bobbing about in the rough swell that hit the reasonably open harbour.

The boat looked small, maybe enough to carry three or four people, a small crabber only, with a red bottom and a compact white wheelhouse on top. It was the only vessel there and Hope decided a call on the radio was the best solution to their woes, as taking the boat to sea in this storm now looked even worse than she had imagined. She also wanted to get a move on as she was beginning to feel cold inside, having sacrificed thermal integrity for clothing she could at least move about in if action was required.

As she coaxed Anders Larsen on, she saw Aldo Brace come along the harbour wall and drop himself onto the boat. He immediately entered the wheelhouse and she watched him turn this way and that. The small window meant she could only see his shoulders and had no idea what he was doing. After a few moments, he exited the wheelhouse and stood on the boat signalling to her with his hands, giving a forlorn gesture.

It took Hope another five minutes to get Larsen to the harbour side with her and she rested him in the shelter of the harbour wall and jumped onto the boat deck.

"It's gone," said Brace. "Some bastard's cut it. The wiring has gone on the radio. We can't use the mic. And I can't see any other way of speaking into it."

Hope brushed by him carefully keeping the man in sight at all times. Picking up the microphone, she saw it had been detached, severed along its cord.

"You're right. Dammit!" Hope made a gesture with the microphone before throwing it onto the floor of the wheelhouse. Then she made a bright smile. "Maybe we could disconnect it and take it to the house I'm sure we have enough bright sparks there who can do something with it."

116

"Good idea," said Brace, "do you know how to disconnect it?"

"Probably," said Hope.

"Okay, well this wheelhouse is too small for two of us to work in comfortably. I'll go and shelter with Larsen while you work on that."

Hope was delighted with this plan and watched him go. The microphone had been severed but she noted that the power was still on to the radio. Giving a quick look up to the harbour wall, she saw Brace sit down beside Larsen. Quickly, Hope looked down at the radio and located the Digital Select Calling distress button. She had seen this in action before on a previous incident she had investigated on a small boat on the Clyde. Basically, this button would send a signal that the Coastguard would pick up, or even another nearby vessel would receive. And it was a distress signal. She pressed it.

All seemed to be fine except the radio made a beeping noise briefly. Hope saw Brace stand up and start to come over. She didn't want to disconnect the mains power because that would stop the signal being sent. But if Brace got close he would see what she was doing. Something in her gut, maybe it was being dumped and ignored due to his homophobia, or maybe it was her police sense, made her want to keep any cry for help away from his ears. After all, he may have cut the microphone.

"Everything all right?" asked Brace jumping on board. Hope pulled at the cable behind the radio.

"Yes, just disconnecting, that's what the beep was. They can make weird sounds, these things, when you mess with the power."

Brace nodded, seemingly happy and climbed back up and over to Larsen who was huddled by the wall. Hope continued

117

with her supposed disconnection of the radio but let it take her a good ten minutes before she actually disconnected it. The signal should have repeated twice by now. Hopefully a VHF aerial would pick up the distress. But would they come in this weather?

Hope eventually appeared back on the harbour side with the radio tucked under her arm. She watched Brace stand up but Larsen was shivering and not just from the cold.

"There's something down there. Looks like another body," said the man, his hands shaking as he pointed towards the end of the harbour wall.

"I can't see anything," said Hope, staring through the snow towards the pier end.

"I think he's right," said Brace, "certainly looks like something to me. You'd better take a look first, Detective; after all, you understand what to do if it is one."

Hope nodded but she was not happy about stepping away from the others. She carefully made her way on the slippery and wet pier, sliding a few times as she neared the end. The sea was crashing up against the wall but it was quite far down. Hope looked behind her to make sure no one was close and able to push her in but the men were back where she had left them. And then she saw Brace take something out of his pocket and cover Larsen's mouth.

Hope turned around to run to Larsen's aid but something had grabbed her ankle. She looked down and there was a tentacle grabbing her like Macaulay had been seized in the upstairs room. It pulled her and she fell to the hard-stone surface and was dragged backwards. Desperately she swam as she hit the water but was pulled down.

Opening her eyes, she could see little and flailed about with her hands. She caught a piece of rock and felt it come away with her as she was pulled downwards. Instinct told her something bad was coming and she placed the rock between her feet. As she was dragged down, she was suddenly flung about and felt something cutting the side of her leg as she twisted in the water. But the pulling had stopped, something below having been damaged by the rock, or so Hope suspected.

Blood was coming from her leg and she felt the salt water nip at the wound. It became pink as blood flowed out but she managed to keep herself moving upwards. As her breath began to run out she broke the surface.

Hope was an extremely competent swimmer but the current conditions in the water were extreme. She fought to keep her head up above the surface and only caught glimpses of the harbour wall which seemed a long distance away. From the occasional glance she could garner, she saw Brace dump Larsen on board the boat and then apparently hull the boat with an axe he had obtained from somewhere. The boat was then untied and allowed to drift off.

Inside Hope raged but as the cold began to take full effect, she decided she needed to come to a plan and quick. The harbour was a long way to swim back to. But the boat was coming her way, drifting off out to sea. Maybe she could do something with it but if it got to the rougher water out at sea, it might even tip over. Still, it was her best bet to get out of the water and then try and keep the boat afloat.

Satisfied that Brace was not looking for her and had started his journey to somewhere else, Hope struck out for the boat. She kept looking up to see if she was still maintaining an intercept course and prayed her legs and body would keep going.

In her mind was the night she had fought the conditions in Lewis and kept a bagged victim afloat. But the water had been calmer then, not the raging tempest it was tonight. And her main concern was how she was going to get on board with the way the swell was throwing her about.

It did not take long for Hope to swim to the boat, helped by swimming across the tide. She arrived at the boat as they were beginning to get into rougher seas. At first, she was thrown up against the boat and desperately flung her hands behind her head as it cracked off the boat. She cried out for Larsen but there was no response.

Now, as she floated in the water, she waited for the swell to fling her at the boat again but this time she kicked to rise with the water and managed to find a purchase with her hands. She clung on desperately as the water descended and left her dangling. Hope swung her feet against the boat and managed to get some purchase so that as the boat was thrown to one side, she was flung with it and fell into the vessel.

Hope rolled onto her back and then into Anders Larsen who was out cold on the deck, which was now about two inches deep in water. Making sure Larsen's face was clear of the water, Hope then staggered into the wheelhouse and looked around. She found the engine panel and tried to start the boat. There was nothing, no noise. And then she checked the aft of the vessel and saw no outboard engine. She was sure there had been one before.

Before panic set in, Hope opened the hatches around the main panels and delved into the depths of the compartments below. Her hands touched blades, the curved whirring kind that can form a propulsion. She pulled the object up and found a small emergency outboard motor. It would struggle in this weather but might keep them from going further out to sea.

Scrabbling in the dark of the compartment, she believed she had found screws and fixtures for the motor and made her way to the aft of the boat. Within a minute, she had secured the motor and dipped the propeller into the water. Now she pulled on the starter. Nothing. Come on! Again nothing. The harbour was getting hard to view through the snow. Hope looked to the sky and swore. It had to work.

Chapter 14

"Mr Smith, with me. We need to find that room upstairs." Macleod pointed at the young man who seemed in shock. "Now, Smith! We need to find where Johnston has gone."

Macleod waited for the younger man to react and then followed him out of the library, along the hallway, and then up a flight of stairs. They ran down another hallway and then Smith stopped abruptly.

"There should be a door here. This was an office suite, a place where Mr Macaulay would work. Inspector, there was a door right here."

Macleod looked at the panelling before him and could see no deviations from the solid wood that ran along the hallway. Pictures adorned the wall but he could see no seam or doorway. Desperately, Macleod ran his hands along the wall and tried to find any imperfection that indicated something false but he saw none.

"Take me round to where this room would be." Macleod saw Smith's blank face. "Where the room is, take me to all sides of it, so I can try and find an entrance."

The light dawned on Smith and he tore off along corridors. They first checked what would be the east side of the room, as best could be told but again there was no access. The south side had a room against it but on searching the wall of that room Macleod saw no obvious way to break through. Now on the west side, Macleod was faced with another hallway devoid of a door where there should be one.

"Doors to rooms beyond the one we need but none into this one. Blast it! Have you a set of ladders, Smith? One that would reach up into that hole in the library ceiling. We could access from below and then find the way out." The man nodded. "Grab them and meet me in the library." Macleod suddenly reached for the man. "Actually, don't do that. Back to the library first."

As he entered the library, Macleod saw Melanie Blayney trying to pull chairs together and construct a rough climbing frame to access the ceiling. Across the room, Mrs Johnston was sitting on a chair crying and was being comforted by Miss Baxter. Pandie was staring up into the open void above him, Zara Dawson standing at his side. From the far door came Mrs Smith with a cup of something hot which she was taking to Mrs Johnston. The look of relief on the woman's face was palatable when she saw her son behind Macleod.

"Okay, Smith, take your mother and grab those ladders for me, please," requested Macleod before making his way directly towards Melanie Blayney. "I appreciate the intent but I have ladders coming."

"Thought it best not to hang around, Inspector. You were obviously having difficulty getting in from above."

"There's no door, no access at all, it's been built around, in similar fashion to the control room, wherever that is. I thought being together in this room would be safer but apparently it is not."

Melanie Blayney smiled at Macleod and flashed a subtle grin at him. "You are trying to look after everyone and I get that. As a private investigator, I'm more used to approaching things directly, being at the source."

"Do not worry, Miss Blayney. I am not just concerned with people's safety. I have two dead, maybe more, so I will get the bastard that has caused this. But we need a lot of thought and not just action. And as loathsome as you private snoopers are, at least I know your motives and I need a wing man with McGrath off gallivanting."

He gave a smile back and Miss Blayney nodded her ascent. It was another five minutes before the ladder arrived, during which time Macleod tried to look up into the room above him without any new revelations. The creature, presumably mechanical, was beyond sight and there was nothing to give away that the room had been filled with a technological piece of wizardry.

The ladder was placed underneath the hole in the ceiling and secured. Macleod asked Pandie to place a foot on it while he climbed up but a hand was placed on his shoulder.

"Wingmen tend to go first into the unknown. We're expendable, you see. Can't have a man of your stature coming to an untimely end." She actually squeezed his shoulder as she said it and then brushed past him closely before stepping onto the ladder. The woman certainly knew how to use her sexuality, which was in abundance, but Macleod did not trust it and saw it for the tool it was.

"Okay, but slowly, we don't want to walk into anything else up there."

Macleod watched Melanie skip up the ladder and then stop just as her head was reaching the level of the ceiling. He heard her gasp and then edge slightly onto her haunches while maintaining a grip on the rungs with her hands.

"There's still something up here. That thing that grabbed Mr Johnston is in the corner of the room. There's a smashed window and that's letting some light in but otherwise it's dark and that thing is simply sitting in the corner. Its stomach is moving."

"Come down," said Macleod, "I'll go in."

"Nonsense, Inspector, not much of a wingman if I don't take on what we find."

Macleod felt the anger rising. This was his show and he should be the one up there. In the force he was used to obeying and being obeyed when giving out definite instructions. *I don't mind a bit of latitude but I have just called it and Melanie Blayney needs to come to heel. Blast, I can't say that these days, probably get accused of being sexist.*

The Welsh woman was now climbing the ladder again and was about to step onto the broken floor above.

"Careful," cried Macleod and stepped onto the ladder behind her and began climbing at pace. He had to get up there and take charge before she did something stupid to herself. Not that he knew what that was, but as she was not following instruction, it could be serious.

The room above was indeed dark except for the light coming through the smashed window. Another window had a blind drawn over it. In the corner a creature was sitting on its rear, breathing heavily. Macleod could barely believe his eyes as the chest rose and fell gently. The thing had pointed ears and a dark leathery skin but the head had eyes that were closed and teeth protruding from its mouth. It was hard to tell in the light but there appeared to be blood on its lips.

"Do you think that's real?" asked Miss Blayney.

"Have you ever seen one before?" asked Macleod. "We had the latex decapitated figures in our first encounter and then a fake body in the cave. So, no I don't think it's real but that doesn't mean it's not harmful so be careful."

To his alarm, Miss Blayney picked up a book that was lying on the wreckage of the floor and threw it at the creature. For a moment Macleod's heart sank until he realised the stupidity of his fear. It was an animated puppet of some sort. And he watched the book bounce off and make a dull noise as it hit the floor.

"Don't go closer yet," Macleod advised, and clambered up the last rungs onto the floor beside the hole in the ceiling. The floor was in remarkably strong condition, or so it appeared, something Macleod thought unnatural. He had experience of falling through weaker floors when he was on a case in Lewis, and although this felt good, he was still feeling like caution was the best route.

But Miss Blayney was having none of it and now marched across the room, straight up to the creature and slapped it. "Yes, you're right. Latex, or something similar. But still, that is some job to make it look that good. And look at this stuff on the floor."

The woman bent down and started showing Macleod some vials of different powders and then a book with markings Macleod would have described as workings of witchcraft. Miss Blayney seemed fascinated by it all and then began looking at paintings in the room, which were grotesque and full of strange creatures.

"Incredible, just amazing. All this trouble to kill someone. Why did Macaulay go to all this trouble? And have himself killed."

"I don't think he did," said Macleod. "Yes, he went to a lot of trouble but I believe he was simply running a horror weekend of sorts. If he wanted a grandstand removal from this life, his was not a success. And why kill off other people? You got to this weekend via him—did he ever seem that crazy? Excitable, yes, but not a lunatic who was happy to kill off others as he went. He seemed a normal, if enthusiastic, role player."

"But look at this stuff, Inspector. It's incredible."

"No, Miss Blayney, don't. Look for the body."

"Johnston?"

"Yes," said Macleod, "where is Mr Johnston? The role-play was for someone to be captured and then presumably eaten. But in reality, that person would be removed to an off-scenario room. Somewhere to remain while the role-play continued. If Johnston was a victim, we should see his body somewhere. If he's in on it, this is a nice way to escape and operate without eyes being on him. And that stays between you and me."

"Mrs Johnston, downstairs; I get you, Inspector."

"And Pandie. If he thought she was involved then we could have a fracas or worse on our hands. So keep it between us, Miss Blayney."

"Okay Inspector, but it's Mel, or Melanie if you prefer. I doubt you call Detective McGrath by her surname." She grinned at him. "I can see why you chose her to be your partner."

"I didn't choose McGrath. We were forced together due to the sickness of a colleague. And yes, I requested she stay working with me because of talents. She's an excellent detective, strong and fast in a situation, unlike me, and sees things differently to my perception of life. We make a good team."

"And she's got a hot booty, too." Macleod raised his eyebrows. "Don't worry," continued Miss Blayney, "it's normal, and she is quite a woman, if you catch my drift."

Macleod did catch her drift but he thought *catch* was the wrong term. He was hit by the juggernaut of her drift, like he was standing in the middle of a motorway unable to move as traffic approached.

Miss Blayney came close and ran her fingers under Macleod's chin. "And I can see why she works with you."

This was harder to ignore. In life, compliments for Macleod were not forthcoming from many people due to his sombre view of life and serious attitude of many years. Even as he had been freed from that after starting to come to terms with his wife's death, he was still withdrawn in daily life. Jane had only broken down so many barriers—others still stood. So to have a woman, and one who looked like Miss Blayney did, come close and compliment in an overtly sexual fashion, was hard to reject off hand. Better to enjoy the moment and then forget it once she had turned away.

"And do I call you Seoras?" asked Miss Blayney, a loose hand dropping from Macleod's chin to his chest.

"Whatever you like, Melanie, as long as you follow my lead."

"As provocative as that sounds, I think we should just get on with the case."

Provocative? How was I provocative? And the case? It's not a television show. And then Macleod found himself self-checking, stopping his thoughts. *She's a player, and a good one.*

"Of course, you are correct, Melanie. Now how do we get out of here? Or more accurately, how did Johnston get out of here?"

A head emerged through the floor. Pandie looked around and then having spotted the investigators asked, "Do you require any help? Have you found him? Mrs Johnston's quite worried. Actually, she's beside herself."

"He's not here, Pandie. As daft as that seems he's not here. So, let her know that but also caution her that doesn't mean he's okay. We simply can't find him."

Pandie nodded and descended the ladder. Melanie Blayney was now running her fingers along the wall furthest from the window, seeking out some defect or opening. Macleod stood close to the middle of the room and looked around. He saw the many pictures, the position of the items on the floor, where the creature was now sitting, and where the attention of the eye would be drawn.

"There's no escape panel on the wall, Melanie, you can stop looking."

The blonde-haired woman spun round and gave a questioning look to Macleod. "How do you know?"

"You jumped straight in, looking for your quick solution. Secret panel to escape from. But look at the room, stand with me and let your eye be drawn to the detail of what's here." Macleod let Melanie join him in the centre of the room and she deliberately stood in front of him, closer than Macleod would have liked. "Now what can you see?"

"There's the creature, the items on the floor, the broken window. I can see the paintings that are really shocking—they grabbed my eye straight away. Then the panelling that looks so neat and complete. Makes you wonder where the door is. But you can't see any door in the panelling. So where do you go?"

"But the ceiling is dull."

"Yes," said Miss Blayney, "most of the other ceilings have ornate decoration or some kind but not this one. It just has two lights, one in the centre and one in the corner, to light up those paintings."

"And what does that make you think?"

Miss Blayney leaned back into Macleod and her hair actually touched his face as she turned her head slightly bringing her face uncomfortably close to his. "Tell me, Seoras."

"That light is wrong. Or at least warrants investigation. You would have a light in the middle of the room but the other one is an afterthought at best, or something more sinister. Maybe the door's in the ceiling?"

Miss Blayney smiled before running across the room and standing under the light. "I don't see anything," she said.

"You need to open the door. In the absence of a handle try and find one. There's not a lot of choice as far as I can see."

"The light itself," Miss Blayney said, and then jumped up and grabbed the hanging fixture. It came down in her hand producing an opening as a panel attached to the light swung down. A rope ladder descended to the ground."

As Macleod walked over to the new opening, Miss Blayney simply stood under it, her hand on her hip smiling. "Nice work, Inspector, shall I go on up?" Macleod nodded and she put a foot on the first rung. But then she turned back to him.

"We make a good team, Seoras. You're a great teacher." Her hand moved to his cheek and gave it a gentle stroke.

"And you, Melanie Blayney, are a player. Kindly get up that ladder and see what you can find. I'll be right up behind you."

As she climbed up the ladder, Macleod tried to not see her jiggling bottom as she climbed. Instead, he looked at the floor and wondered how to play this next passage of time. Discovery of the secret places could bring a killer out in the open and to be more brazen, especially as they did not have the strength of numbers or experience to simply arrest the culprit. Or culprits. Something was kicking at him, some notion. As much as Miss Blayney had the outside image of Hope, she was not the detective his colleague was. And right now, he wished Hope was with him.

Chapter 15

A sick feeling was coming up Hope's throat and it had nothing to do with the choppy sea they were on. As she braced her legs, the boat bobbed this way and that and then she saw her compatriot on the vessel, Anders Larsen tumbled forward and hit his head hard on the deck. But she ignored him, desperately pulling on the cord of the motor. Was it simply disuse, or was it broken? She prayed for the former. A glance told her the harbour was disappearing at too fast a rate.

And then there came a spark of life. The motor turned over briefly. She pulled at it again and there was nothing. So Hope pulled again. "Come on, you bastard. Don't you dare think about lifting my hopes just to ram them back down my throat." Hope pulled on the chord and this time it turned over, and then kept turning.

Her mood suddenly lifted, she put her cold nose into the wind and looked for a course to steer. Where would Aldo Brace make for? If he was still at the harbour he could be waiting. Although what was his plan? To return and kill more people. Hope shivered. She was freezing cold stuck out in the worst storm in a while but thankfully they had not made it to the really rough water. They were still in the protection of an outcrop and the waves were subdued because of this. Much further and the boat would not be much use.

But there was another problem. Aldo Brace had damaged the boat's integrity with an axe. Thankfully, he had made a ham-fisted job of it and water was coming in at a slow, if not exactly safe, rate. But someone had to keep the boat on a straight course and someone else was needed to bail out the water that was coming in.

"Anders, Anders! Wake the hell up, Anders." There was nothing from the Scandinavian. "Bollocks to that, Anders, and wake up! I need you!"

Hope had heard the crack of his skull as he hit the deck and had winced at the sound. Poor guy was probably not in a good way but first things first. She had to get the boat to shore before doing anything else. But maybe he could help.

Hope left the motor momentarily and stepped over to the man, grabbing him from behind under the armpits. From here she staggered with the motion of the boat before dropping Karlsen beside the motor's steering handle. She adjusted him and placed his arm over the tiller and made it line up roughly with the harbour. It would need to be checked once they had got going to account for the tide but it might work.

She looked at the man once he was set in position and she noted he was breathing. That was all he was doing, however, and so she set to the task of scooping water out of the boat. In the compartments in the wheelhouse, she found a small plastic container and started to bail the water out. But she was cold. And Anders Karlsen must be as well. Surely she could find something to help cover him because at the moment the going was slow and they could be out here for an hour or two.

Returning to the wheelhouse, she found some sheeting and

draped it over the prone man. Once complete, she went back to her tub and the emptying of incoming water. But her brain was engaging on other problems.

What was this they were in? Who was responsible and how do you set it up? Had their late arrival really screwed things up and the perpetrator decided to act as if everything was normal and just kill off whoever? Was there even an agenda here?

Aldo Brace was clearly involved but what was his role? Solo lunatic? If so, how did he affect the machinery? He was in the USA playing rugby recently and he had been at matches in Europe before that.

If he was in a squad of killers then what was his role and why were they doing it? Brace clearly had a problem with non-heterosexual relationships but was that it? Peter McKinney was homosexual and he had been the first to die. But his partner Pandie was the real activist. But then just how far could actions be controlled? There was a craziness in this as well. What a crazy way to kill people? Couldn't they just use a gun?

The water was still coming in and Hope thought the rate was increasing. So far, the boat was struggling with the small motor to make much headway back to shore. Maybe the currents would be easier further along the shore. She had to remain close as drifting further out was definitely going to bring wave heights she was sure the boat would struggle with. However, if they stayed out here too long, she would get hyperthermia and who knew just how Anders Larsen's body was coping?

Hope shifted Larsen slightly and adjusted the tiller until the vessel was pointing to the outcrop that was providing the shelter from the elements' full fury. There was no harbour and plenty of rock around what seemed to be a small beach but she'd have to risk it. It was more important to get to land and shelter.

She heard a moan from the aft of the boat and when she looked Larsen's head rolled to one side. Hope dropped her makeshift plastic scoop and knelt down in front of the man. His blond hair was blowing with the wind and his eyes were flicking open as if he was trying to come around.

"Larsen, Anders Larsen, can you hear me?" asked Hope.

The man murmured slightly before staring at her with eyes that showed he was not fully coherent. She slapped him lightly on the cheek and was taken with how cold his cheek was. Regardless, he was awake and she needed to keep him conscious and as alert as he could be.

"Listen Anders, we are in the boat and Aldo has set us on the sea. The boat's taking on water and I'm trying to get us back to land because if we don't, we'll drown when the boat sinks. Can you hear me, Anders?"

"Cold." It was just the one word but he said it over and over again. And then he broke into a Nordic language, possibly Swedish. Hope tried to talk again but the man was babbling now, or at least as much as his chattering teeth would allow. *I need to get to shore fast*, thought Hope, *and get him inside*.

Hope looked out at the shore and was lifted by the sight of it being somewhat nearer. But the boat was still taking water and she went back to bailing out. Over the next hour, she fought hard to keep the water from flooding the vessel but it was rising and had gone past her ankles and was rising higher. But the shore was in sight.

It was somewhat bizarre, she thought, to be stuck in a sinking vessel with the snow falling all around you. She had pictured herself when younger and in her true days of swimming prowess, diving into the surf to rescue holidaymakers who had been swept off to sea. But those dreams were on beaches were the sun kissed the sand and Hope spent as much time looking magnificent in the bronzed cohort of rescuers as she did saving lives. Now she was in a nightmare and relying on skills that had not disappeared but were rusty.

With the rise of the water, the vessel was beginning to slow its progress. Hope gauged the distance to shore and believed that while it was not guaranteed, it was at least worth the risk to attempt a swim to shore. But she would need to take Larsen with her and was putting her own life into greater jeopardy than just swimming herself. Alone, she believed she would make it nine times out of ten but with a passenger, who knew the odds.

He needed buoyancy. Hope scoured the boat and then the compartments for a lifejacket but there were none. But she found several fenders on the side of the vessel. Untying them, she took their ropes and tied them to Larsen keeping the link as short as possible. It was better than nothing but it was not ideal.

His eyes were glazed as he watched her do this but when she tapped his cheek he looked at her without speaking.

"We're going to swim to shore, Anders. I don't know if this will work but I'll help you, okay? You need to swim if you can or else just hold tight to the fenders, the floats."

"Cold." It was the only reply but the man stood up when Hope prompted him. With the sheeting removed, Hope could see his legs shaking with cold and she wondered if this was really the best option. But then again, she could not see another viable solution, if indeed this was viable. It was a chance. Only a chance.

With another section of rope, Hope tied the man to herself giving a bit of slack on the rope so he would not impede her swimming. "You need to try and float, let the fenders keep you up," Hope advised but she was unsure just how much he understood or could comply with. She put her arms around his waist and lifted him onto the edge of the boat. The vessel pitched suddenly and Anders fell into the water. Hope dived in before the rope pulled her in.

The cold of the water came as a surprise given how cold she thought she already was. For a moment she treaded water and kept her head above, sucking in air in as calm a manner as she could muster. She had no buoyancy aid on herself preferring to cling to Anders if necessary and use his fenders.

With the waves being reasonably high, Hope could only snatch glimpses of the small beach she was heading for. Happy she was over any shock from the cold water, she began to swim towards the shore, but immediately felt the drag of Anders Larsen. She doubted the man was giving any assistance and she was lucky if he was in any shape to even keep himself upright.

She knew she had to focus but she could also feel the panic building, knowing she might not be able to save the man behind her. Was he even conscious or had the cold water affected him? She could be pulling a dead weight, literally.

Hope ignored the idea for a while, continuing on with her swimming trying to concentrate on form and direction, but the nagging doubt remained. As fatigue began in her own arms, she grew more doubtful. The sea was now getting rougher as they approached land and she was buffeted about. Maybe her floating passenger was causing the buffet to be stronger? It felt to Hope she did not have the strength to drag him at this time and that she was being dragged back out instead.

Hope stopped and pulled herself along the rope towards Larsen. As she reached him, her heart sank. The man had flipped over at some point and was now face down in the water. Hope tried to lift the man out of the water but the conditions prohibited it. She grabbed his head and lifted it out of the water but she could see no breathing. Tears began to form in her eyes as she let his head drop.

Hope's mind began to cloud. She could not leave him here. What about his family? What about the investigation? He needed a post mortem, needed to show the damage before he drowned. A thousand images ran across her mind before she remembered to breathe. In cold water, breathe, stay calm. *Stay flaming calm, Hope!*

She reached down and started to untie the rope around her waist. As she bobbed back up on a wave she saw Larsen's head, face down, and said a quiet "Sorry" to the air. The rope slipped away and she turned back to shore. *Don't think, Hope, just do.*

Without her passenger, Hope felt herself moving quicker through the water. Nothing ran through her mind as her whole focus was made on every stroke and kick. Concentrating on her form gave her a purpose and a barrier to a wandering mind she knew was just around the corner. But it was still a race to get to shore and then a race for shelter.

As the waves broke around her, Hope smiled inside. She was close to shore, close to safety. She felt herself thrown forward and a foaming mass surrounded her. She was close to the beach. Letting herself rotate to a standing position she found the sand beneath her feet. But a wave knocked her off her feet and she tumbled forward, water racing up her nose. Extending both arms, she managed to lift her head up above water and found herself yards from the beach. With a mighty effort, she stood and stomped the last few steps to the beach where she collapsed on the ground and gasped for air.

And then the tears flowed. Larsen was gone, she had got to him but he was gone. Aldo Brace's face came to mind. She had told Macleod this was survival; well, here she was and she was coming for Brace.

And then she laughed, crazily, inappropriately but heartily. *Coming for him, I'm frozen, exhausted and in need of help. There must be something round here because I need heat. Come on, girl, get your arse into gear or you'll be dead, too.*

Hope stood up—unsteadily—but upright into the wind. There was a determination inside to see Brace behind bars. Occasionally, it became a little more than that but she reminded herself she was a police officer and a conviction would have to do. Now where was she going?

As she traipsed up the beach, she saw the white of the snow beyond. She needed to go right, the house was to the right as you looked at the beach. She could hug the shoreline but there were two issues there. No shelter until the house and also Brace might be there. She was in no condition to take him on if she ran into him. When she had looked at the area on-line, there had been a road running from the house.

Hope struck out from the beach across what seemed like a field. There was no heather showing, so deep was the snow, and she felt it come up to her ankles. But then she saw a white shape sticking out above the main level of the ground. As quick as she could she ran to the shape and found a car with a small snow drift on its lee side. Hope ran around to the other side and tried the door. It opened. She clambered inside and felt the immediate relief of being out of the wind. It was shelter

139

but not heat. She leaned across and thanked God as she saw the ignition with keys hanging down. She turned them and the engine stuttered. Another turn and the engine started.

Every heating dial was turned to full and Hope waited for the heat to kick in. It took about five minutes but then there was hot air coming and she turned the direction of the blowers onto herself. But she was still in wet clothes. She checked the back of the car and saw a blanket. The space was tight but Hope stripped and wrapped herself in the blanket. She lay down across the seats in the front and found herself beginning to nod off. With her last thought, she saw Brace returning to the house, giving some fake story about how Larsen and she had died. And then she saw Macleod's face. She needed to get back to him. But then she fell asleep, exhaustion finally overtaking her.

Chapter 16

Macleod watched Miss Blayney climb the rope ladder and enter through the hatch in the ceiling. The ladder had swung here and there as she climbed and he was not looking forward to climbing it after her. He walked back to the large hole in the floor and shouted to those still in the library that he was going to be a while as they had found something further to investigate.

"Pandie, Mr Smith, keep an eye on everyone and if needs be, move to another room but stay together. I would say come with us but that might not be so easy looking at where we are going."

"There's a small private room used by the master, or was used by him, sorry," said Mr Smith. "It has a small fireplace and would be warm. It might also be safer if he didn't expect anyone to be using it."

"Okay," said Macleod, "but be careful and stay together. We'll be as quick as we can."

Grabbing the swinging ladder, Macleod gingerly climbed up into the gap in the ceiling. As his head came through the gap, it met the face of Miss Blayney.

"Seoras, there's a tunnel, or a passage of some sort but we'll have to crawl along it. Looks big enough to do it on our knees but it's also quite dark. Stay close behind me."

The voice did not sound that keen for the task at this point and Macleod understood. He doubted Melanie Blayney was used to chasing down killers and the thought she could be crawling into a trap or real danger was not one he was overly happy about either. But the chase was on now, they had a foothold in the door and he was sure he was not going to back off. She probably felt the same way.

"I'm right with you. No risks, though," said Macleod.

"This is kind of risky, Seoras. I think we left that idea behind when we climbed up here."

She was right, of course, and Macleod simply gave a smile that he hoped would bolster her confidence. It felt odd because despite the fact she was a private investigator, she was still a civilian to him. But Hope had said survival and so maybe she was an equal here. They both wanted to survive.

He watched Miss Blayney start to shuffle along the narrow corridor above the ceiling and threw himself into the passageway behind her. The light was extremely poor and he could just about make out her shoes. And then a green, low intensity light came on, like that displayed by emergency lights in a crisis. He could see along the corridor, at least enough to move confidently but Miss Blayney was still indistinct, more of a shape than a defined figure, like a blurred photograph. Some of this might have been due to his own long sightedness.

The passageway started moving further into the house before it reached a junction. Miss Blayney stopped abruptly and Macleod was right behind her so could see the choice ahead.

"Do you have any ideas on which path to follow?" she asked.

"Are there any marks, any indications on the sides of the

passage? Any shoe scuffs on the floor?"

"None, Seoras. I guess it's pot luck."

"Yes, it is, but if we think about it, and we assume Macaulay was heading for a control room on the night he died, then that control room would more than likely be towards the right."

"Good point, Seoras. So, we'll go that way."

"Yes." And it was at that point Macleod realised he was speaking in a different tone to the woman than he would speak to Hope or anyone in the force. He must sound like a patronising oaf. "And Miss Blayney, my apologies if I sound like a schoolmaster teaching his pupil. I'm not being sexist, just trying to explain in a rather half-baked effort."

"Don't worry Seoras, I'm sure you're a pompous arse to everyone. And I'm sorry if I flirted quite hard on you. Some men are easier to control that way when you need something. I can see you're not. But frankly, you are my best chance of getting out of here alive, so I needed to be around you."

"Flattery will get you everywhere," said Seoras. *And if I didn't have such a good woman in Glasgow it might have been more effective.* "Let's get on, Melanie. Right, it is."

Following Miss Blayney along the tunnel, he saw another divergence up ahead but this time they found a short, stubby off-shoot that ended abruptly. Miss Blayney allowed Macleod to come up alongside and he felt the floor where the off-shoot stopped.

"I thought there would be a drop-down piece into another room, and hopefully the control room. But I can't see anything."

"Back up Seoras, and let me take a proper look. I've dealt with a lot of catches and door mechanisms in my line of work. I doubt you break into many places." He caught an indistinct

143

smile in the poor light and slid back to allow her a clear area to work in. Watching her sweep her hands around, Macleod realised that she had obviously built this skill up over time and it was less than a minute before she found a subtle mechanism in the wall.

"You can hardly see it, but it's there. I think he didn't want anyone who actually got into this tunnel to get into any of the other rooms."

"It would ruin Macaulay's games," said Macleod, "but also handy for whoever has taken it over from him. But it confirms my suspicions that the killer must have been in on the build with Macaulay."

Miss Blayney pressed up against the wall and a hatch slid away in front of her. "Ready for this room?"

Macleod nodded. "Slowly and watch out. It'll probably be a trap but an altered one." He watched her nod and look at him with serious eyes, not the sparkling ones he had become used to from her. "I'll be close, Melanie. And you keep an eye on me."

Miss Blayney peered down into the room which was dark but another rope ladder was descending down into the blackness. Swinging herself round, she gave Macleod a smile and then began to descend. Macleod, on his knees, peered into the room, spying for any traps or dangers that may be there. Satisfied she had reached the bottom of the ladder safely, he climbed down as well.

The room was extremely different to the rest of the house and there was a large desk and a conference type table. The rope ladder had descended close to the wall and Macleod ran his hands along it, finding a simple switch which he activated.

Strong white light from strip bulbs on the ceiling bathed

the room in brightness. Around the room were designs on the wall, technical drawings of horrific creatures and fiendish mechanisms. Macleod was out of his depth with the detail but the whole package looked like a lifetime of work.

Miss Blayney cautiously stepped across to the desk that was littered with paper. There was a large green diary sitting on one side amidst three telephones, all of various styles, like some tribute to communication through recent times. She picked up a few of the papers and quickly scanned them.

"Correspondence from the States, Japan, and England here. Mostly about technical things and pricing, I can't see anything that's not related to building these monstrosities in the house."

"Anything in the drawers, Melanie?" asked Macleod. "I don't think anything of note would be on top in case someone came in here. Although there's no doors out—well, any obvious ones. But the furniture must have come in. There's ventilation runs in the wall though so maybe the room is sealed in. Look in the corner, a computer and printers. A sealed in office. Incredibly secretive, not even the staff would be in here."

"Seoras," said Miss Blayney, "in the far corner, do you see the chute?" Furthest from them was a metal hatch with the words "waste disposal on it". There's even a hoover beside it. Not a place for the staff to look after then."

"No," said Macleod, "a real hideaway. Check the drawers."

Macleod started looking though the papers on the large solid conference desk, but they looked like more drawings and operating instructions. There were a few manuals and he saw a number based on panels that were not in the room. And he saw the manual entitled, "Overview" and opened the first page to find a logo of a gnome with a cap on and looking decidedly thoughtful. Below the image were the words "Gimbel Brothers Ltd". Macleod flicked on through the contents and saw drawings of a room containing many panels and control boards. He saw words like "demon", "winged beast" and "false ceiling". This was the overall instruction manual. Although it was clearly a basic overview, Macleod decided to pocket the manual but on trying to fit it into his jacket pocket, he found it too large.

"Got something here, Melanie," he advised. "Operating instructions, or at least an overview. Do you have anything?"

"Just on the third drawer, Seoras. It seems—"

Miss Blayney pitched backwards and collapsed to the floor. Running over, Macleod rounded the desk and saw her lying on her back, sprawled on the floor. He checked her pulse and found it to be strong. Her chest was rising and falling. He opened the eyes that had fallen closed but there showed no recognition. And then he saw the small dart protruding from her shoulder.

A cold chill ran through him as he wondered how to get help to the woman. There were no doors out, just a rope ladder and a crawl along narrow passages. Could he even get her up the ladder on his back? He doubted it. And what was the dart? Poison? A simple knock out dose?

Carefully, Macleod rolled Miss Blayney onto her side and tried to set her up in the recovery position. As far as he could tell, she was merely knocked out, everything else seemed normal. Her temperature was not raised, she was not sweating or chilled. Her limbs moved normally and she breathed regularly. Apart from not responding, she was in decent shape.

Macleod looked at the offending drawer. *Third one down she had said.* Stepping to the side of the drawer Macleod tried pulling it again. A second dart shot out of the desk and landed on the rear wall. A third pull of the drawer received no response but the drawer did not open. *What on earth is in there that you need to protect it in a room that does not exist to the outside world?*

Although he wanted the drawer open, Macleod also knew he was going to struggle to achieve that goal as he had no items with which to attack the drawer. He sat down on a chair and pondered the next course of action. He did not want to leave Miss Blayney alone but he could not take her with him unless she recovered. But that would slow the investigation and who knew who could suffer or be eliminated by that time. But to leave her alone was a serious risk.

He would quickly return and split up the remaining party, leaving some with Miss Blayney and take a few along with him. Macleod took one more look at Miss Blayney before climbing the ladder back to the narrow passageway above. Retracing his steps, he soon returned to the collapsed ceiling that looked into the library.

"Anyone still there?" shouted Macleod. No answer was forthcoming and he descended the ladder to a deserted room. Mr Smith must have moved the party to a different room like he had said and Macleod exited the library and made his way along a new corridor beyond the library. It made sense that they moved but he was not sure to where. Had someone said? He could not remember. It was all so confusing and he tried to focus on what was ahead of him rather than scour his mind for what had been said. The house was dangerous and he needed to be on his game.

Macleod tried the first door he came to and found a closet with coats and wellies. A second door was an opening to a small bathroom. Beyond this door were two others, and

Macleod opened the first. There was a dim red light that meant he could see shadows of figures standing upright. He heard voices, Pandie shouting as he stepped into the room but the man seemed distant, not in the room. He had taken two steps inside when the door swung shut behind him.

Macleod tried to size up what was happening but the light was poor that he could only see the figures ahead of him. They were about his size but the heads were elliptical and seemed to have bulbous eyes. He stepped forward slowly. There came a whooshing sound and he saw the furthest figure being whipped away. Then another sound and the second figure collapsed. A third figure seemed to lose its head as another whooshing sound filled his ears. He heard someone shout, "Macleod, is that you?"

There came a whoosh that was right beside him.

Chapter 17

It was mainly instinct. Whatever else age had brought to Macleod it had not tainted his policeman's instinct which right now made him drop to his knees. Something cut the air above his head and he heard other things hit the floor in the dark room. He froze in the same spot, resting on his haunches, and scanned the remainder of the room.

Several figures were on the floor and a disturbance was occurring on the far wall. He had no other way to describe it but as a swirl in the wall itself. The whole room had only a dark red glow except for this rotating mass of stars highly concentrated on the wall at head height. Something appeared to fly into it and then the whole swirling mass vanished. The dim red glow now intensified and became a strong red light that brought horror to his eyes. Before him he saw creatures like he had seen in the barn. They were decapitated and there was red everywhere, dark and flowing on the floor.

Macleod steeled himself and reached forward to pick up a head. It was latex. *Macaulay was sick,* he thought, *but not as sick as the individual who is playing the game for real*. He heard a voice calling for him and recognised Pandie's voice.

"Can you open the door, Mr McKinney?" said Macleod. He wanted to keep his eyes on the room lest anything else happened when the door was opened again.

"Of course, Inspector, are you all right?"

"I believe so but I really would like to exit the room without further incident. I don't trust it, so if you would open the door that would be most helpful."

Macleod heard the door swing open. He stayed low and surveyed the room. Nothing happened and he turned his head to Pandie who was standing at the door but with Miss Baxter looking over his shoulder. She screamed.

"Don't let the door close, Pandie. Miss Baxter, please step away, none of it's real—all fake, so try to relax."

"Relax!" she yelled. "Your father wasn't a sick bastard. Bloody hell!"

"I need to check the walls, Pandie but I don't want that door to shut, that's very important. Don't let the door shut whatever else happens."

"Understood," said Pandie. "What happened?"

"There was some sort of blade passing about, it was too dark to see clearly. It took the heads off the figures and I think it would have had me but I dropped down before it swung my way. The door closing activated it, so keep the door open."

Pandie gulped and braced himself at the door. Seeing the action, Macleod rose and quickly ran his hands over the wall. There was the thinnest of gaps where something could emerge, maybe a spinning disc? Satisfied that the threat to his life had been real, Macleod turned and exited the room.

"You can close the door, Pandie."

Pandie stepped away and the door shut. From inside there was no noise. And Pandie took Macleod by the shoulder with one hand. "Are you okay? Come through to the kitchen, that's where we all are. Some of us did not feel too safe waiting in the room for you to return. Hey," he said suddenly, "where's Melanie?"

"We ran into a bit of trouble," said Macleod. "She's unconscious but otherwise breathing and somewhere safe. But it was down a rope ladder and I couldn't lift her back out of the room. However, I believe she's in as safe an environment as this house offers."

Miss Baxter walked and stood in front of him, her head bowed, almost inviting him to take hold of her. She was sniffling and did not look up. "Don't leave me, Inspector. I'm scared. Can we not just get out of this house, somewhere? Anywhere?"

Macleod let her fall into his arms and cradled her like a child. If she was acting it was incredibly convincing. Pandie pointed to the other door at the end of the hallway and opened it for Macleod to walk through whilst he held onto the stumbling Miss Baxter.

He walked into a brightly lit kitchen and saw his previous companions spread out around the room. Mr Smith was cooking at a series of gas hobs while the others were generally sitting on various stools. Mrs Johnston was being attended to by Mrs Smith while Zara Dawson was looking out a window.

"My husband? Did you see my husband, Inspector?" asked Mrs Johnston, but her tone was not hopeful.

"No," said Macleod. "But I didn't see him dead either. He's missing. Sorry it's not better news."

The woman bent over and sobbed. Before she had seemed towering, strong, but now she was a mess. Mrs Smith took hold of the woman again and tried to comfort her. "Where's the soup, Kyle?" she asked of her son.

"Coming," said the young man.

"Good idea," said Macleod, "but I need to go back and bring Miss Blayney back here. She was knocked unconscious." This was not true but Macleod did not want to give away where he had been to everyone. He had no idea yet who was to blame for these deaths and he was not about to let the killer know just what he knew, as little as it was. "I should be able to achieve that goal with the assistance of someone strong. Mr Smith, perhaps, or Pandie?"

"I'll go with you, Inspector," said Pandie.

"Let me come too," said Miss Baxter. "I don't feel safe with anyone. But you should be on the side of good, not involved in this."

"How do you know that?" asked Macleod.

"Because my father was upset at the late call up. He had deliberately asked for your boss. Said it would annoy the backer."

Macleod let the comment pass but he was forming a strategy. If he could get back to the room and find something, anything to link someone from this party to the development of the game, then he may have his killer. It was a long shot but he didn't have any other bullets to fire.

My boss, the rising star of the Scottish police force, making waves up the ladder. Who would want her dead? Well, could think of a few criminals but this does not feel like the criminal element here. This feels like something else. Not sure what else, but something. That shower stunt that nearly killed Hope was intended for the boss. She'd thank us because this is above and beyond the call.

"Mr Smith," said Macleod, "I'm placing you in charge here. Look after Mrs Johnston, your mother and Miss Dawson. Stay safe and no risks. Stay in here and lock the doors if you can. Make sure you have food, use the heat, and stay safe. Oh, and get me an axe. That's all, am I understood?"

"Yes, Inspector. What are your plans?" asked Mr Smith.

"We'll go and get Miss Blayney and then, first, bring her here. She'll need assistance. Beyond that I'm going to find who is behind this. I'm tired of waiting around to be picked off. I'm going to find and arrest this piece of evil that's after us. Mr McKinney is coming to assist me and I may need Miss Dawson. She's very nimble, I'm told. Personally, Miss Baxter wants to come with me, but I think this place will be safer. And that's my final decision," he said as Miss Baxter rose to protest.

Mrs Johnston stood up and came over to Macleod in tears. "Find my husband. Even if he's . . ."

Macleod nodded. "I will, ma'am. I'll also find who's responsible. Please go sit down. Mrs Smith, please take over."

Macleod was not the greatest with weeping victims, being happier on the hunt or facing the evil he sought. But he did feel for the woman. He was also feeling concern for Hope, but he had his side of the investigation to focus on. Outside, he heard the storm still raging. Would there be no end of it?

"One axe, sir," announced Mr Smith.

Taking it in his hand, Macleod felt the weight of the head and the balance of it. If he had to use this as a weapon it was going to be hard work. With his small party, Macleod retraced his steps to the library and then up through the ceiling, along the small passageways and then down the rope ladder into the office without a door.

"Crikey," said Pandie. "This is where he dreamed the whole thing up from. I can't believe that he managed to keep all this quiet." Then he saw Miss Blayney on the floor. "What happened to her? Is she okay? She's moving."

Macleod pushed in front of Pandie and dropped to one knee

153

in front of Miss Blayney. She was trying to sit up and she almost fell back before Macleod caught her.

"Seoras," she murmured. "Thank God, Seoras. What was that?"

"Dart of some sort. Triggered when you tried to open the drawer. I've set the others off so it's safe. In fact, Pandie's going to break the drawer open. Go on then, Pandie."

Supporting Miss Blayney's head, Macleod watched Pandie take to his work with glee. The man obviously knew how to swing an axe and he had destroyed the front of the drawer in a matter of a minute.

"Okay, Pandie, good work." Macleod took some documents from the drawer. "Hey, Miss Dawson, look through these." He gave some of the others to Pandie. "You too, Pandie, see if there's anything interesting."

He sat himself down and Miss Blayney propped herself up on him. Together they examined the remaining documents. Macleod wasn't sure if she was functioning fully but he wanted to keep her mind active. But to his astonishment she pointed to a paragraph with her finger.

"This letter—it's quite pointed, Seoras. And that writing in the middle, that's not English or any other European language. Mrs Johnston is your woman for that. But there's also someone insisting that the Chef Inspector makes it to the evening, quite insistent. Is that your boss, Seoras, the one you replaced here?"

Macleod nodded. This was becoming very personal and he was trying to keep a clear head. Something was wrong. This was an execution then if people were brought here by design. Not a madman but someone deluded. But about what? What had his boss done recently or in the past to draw attention to this? She was a model officer. And the guidelines were there to follow so she did not set the rules. Instead, maybe it was what she represented but surely there would be easier ways to showcase that thought.

"Anything from your papers?" Macleod asked Pandie and Miss Dawson.

"I don't fully understand the words, but here's someone saying that I needed to come and to do all necessary to bring me here," said Miss Dawson.

"Is it dated?" asked Macleod.

"That's good," said Miss Blayney but Macleod wasn't listening.

"It's three months ago," replied Miss Dawson.

"When did you accept your invite for here?" asked Macleod.

"I didn't. It was Aldo who said we should come. I'm just tagging along; it was his idea."

"There's nothing in my papers I can make out that would be useful," said Pandie.

"Okay," said Macleod and then nudged Miss Blayney when she went to speak. "We'll get back to the kitchen and see if Mrs Johnston can bring us up to speed on this. I've also got a manual for the whole scheme but it's very entry level. I'll see if Smith can help me fathom where things are going."

Miss Blayney refused help but placed herself beside Macleod as they waited to follow Pandie and Zara up the rope ladder. "Aldo said to come?" she whispered. "Do you think she's in danger?"

"We all are, Melanie. But I wish I could talk to Mr Brace right now. There are connections being dangled but I need more. It's maybe time to gather for dinner, see what a chin wag can offer."

Chapter 18

Back in the kitchen, Macleod tasked Mr Smith with making something to eat and set his small team of mainly scared individuals to work. They had brought the papers from the locked drawer back with them and he had given Pandie and Miss Dawson charge of looking through them further. He was sitting at a table with Mrs Johnston and Miss Baxter looking over the letter Miss Blayney had seen as important. He felt he could best assist on this as he was the only one in the room who actually knew his boss.

"The language is Egyptian, Inspector," said Mrs Johnston but it is unlikely to be modern. The language is older and yet used very clumsily. It is as if they did not know the language but had picked it up from a phrase book. Like an Englishman wandering the streets with his Russian guidebook but not actually having had any previous contact or immersion in the language."

"How do you mean?" asked Macleod. "Or rather for what purpose?"

"If I was to guess," continued Mrs Johnston, "I would be thinking that someone needed to believe he or she was being clever, or had something to hide, or at least give that impression. But anyone who can read basic Egyptian could read this, despite the obvious abuse of the language."

"And it says?" asked Miss Baxter.

"It talks of *The Pure Vine*. That's the repeated name given although it does not relate what that is; however, I would surmise it is a group or band of people from the context. But there's little that is sinister here. Simply a determined exhortation to bring your boss to the weekend gathering and saying that funding is dependent on it and on the other factors being in place too."

"Okay, that's interesting but not very damning or revealing of anyone. Would you be so kind as to look through the other papers with me, Mrs Johnston? In fact, can Miss Baxter and you make a start while I catch up with everyone else?"

Having been given Mrs Johnston's agreement, Macleod checked on Miss Blayney who was lying on the floor with a blanket under her head. She had her eyes closed but flicked them open as Macleod stood above her.

"How goes it, Inspector?" said Miss Blayney. "Found anything juicy?"

"Not much. Does *The Pure Vine* mean anything to you?"

"No, never heard of it."

"It appears they, whoever they are, had something to do with building this monstrosity of a weekend and for bringing, or at least attempting, to bring my boss here. Like me, they failed to succeed in making her go somewhere she didn't want to. Miss Blayney smiled at the joke. "Are you feeling any better?"

"Yes," she replied, "the headache has nearly gone. Still a little out of sorts but should be able to get up and help soon."

"Take it easy. We're going to eat and I'm still scanning these papers. Also, I need to interview some of the guests more intensely and try to find some connections. So, lie down until we at least eat."

Macleod watched her nod and then close her eyes. As he turned away, he realised he was developing a fondness for Miss Blayney. Despite her excellent figure and looks, this was not what was grabbing his feelings. Rather she had a feisty and determined disposition that was giving him a closeness to her that was maybe undeserved. He needed to watch what bias this created as he was truly unsure of everyone in this party except Hope.

He had expected Hope to be back by now but knew sending her out had been a risk. With so much to do and the lives of everyone in the house at risk he had simply left the outside plan to her. He hoped he did not regret that.

Mr Smith announced lunch and his mother placed several bowls of soup on the table along with bread. Macleod was famished and ate hungrily once he had seen Smith taste the soup. There was no need to be reckless just because you were hungry.

He managed to sit beside Miss Dawson who looked pale and somewhat nervous. As he tucked into his soup, she played with her spoon and then asked Macleod straight out, "Do you think Aldo is involved in this?"

"I don't know, Miss Dawson. What's he like as a person?" asked Macleod.

"He's been very charming as long as I have known him, which isn't long. My folks were not happy I was seeing him but then they still think I'm a child and that I need to concentrate more on my gymnastics than be with Aldo. He works out almost daily with his rugby but because we live quite close we've been able to see a lot of each other."

"How did you meet?"

"Well, that is funny because we don't really move in the same circles. Yes, we are both athletes but the gymnastic squad is very close knit and stays quite enclosed. We were on an intensive two week burst at the university, using their facilities, and Aldo was there working rehab in the gym with his personal physio. I would be in the gym from time to time and he came over to chat. He can be quite delightful. Really grabbed me by the heart, Inspector."

"He *can* be delightful?" queried Macleod. "Does he have moments?"

"He's very passionate about things. Has certain standards. I think that comes from his church upbringing. He goes every Sunday. I back a charity that helps people who have difficulty with living their life for who they are due to intimidation and abuse. I was attending a rally they were having and Sarah Bale was going to be the main speaker."

"I don't really know who you are talking about?" said Macleod.

"Maybe that's because it was in America, Inspector. She won a discrimination case against her employers at a beer firm. She had been their main marketing image until she came out as being a transvestite. Aldo didn't say much about my going to the event but I could tell he wasn't happy. And he didn't go. He's come to everything else I have done, except this charity of mine. Weird. But he's been lovely, really, Inspector. I could not have hoped for a more perfect boyfriend. It was the least I could do coming with him to this, although the place had been giving me the creeps even before the killings started. Now I don't know who to trust."

You're not alone there, thought Macleod. "What did your folks think of you coming over here with Mr Brace?"

"Well, they were not happy. I'm meant to be training but I faked a bit of a strain. Figured I owed Aldo this one as he was so insistent on coming here."

Miss Baxter came over to Macleod and simply stood beside him while he was talking to Miss Dawson until he turned to acknowledge her. "Sorry, Inspector but can we talk?"

"Of course, Miss Baxter."

"Alone?"

Macleod excused himself from the table and walked with Miss Baxter to the far end of the kitchen and then said in a whisper, "What is it?"

"What has my father done? He was involved in all this? I mean, all those papers you brought down, the foreign writing, this crazy building he made."

Macleod shook his head. "I simply don't know about your father yet. But I think he was genuine in his desire for a horror weekend. Did he do anything like this before? You seemed to think so, when you saw the building at the rear of the house. All the latex creatures and fake blood. Or rather pig's blood."

"He's been fascinated by the macabre all his life but this is something different. He would go to conventions, be in role-play sessions, that is, sorry, was part of him." Miss Baxter sniffed and fought to continue. "It drove my mother mad before she died as he seemed happier in his fantasy worlds than with her. He would have loved all this. Well you saw him when he arrived."

"Indeed, very animated, but killers get animated too, Miss Baxter."

"But my dad was not like that. He was gentle. Yes, he had some strong views at times but he was always one who liked the debate, not any direct action on people. He was quite old fashioned when it came to relationships and lifestyles; his papers even carried some pieces against this new wave of sexuality but he always said that society had to be inclusive too, if that was what the people voted for."

"Did he show any particular aggression against anyone?" asked Macleod.

"Only me. He said I was promoting too many dodgy causes on my morning show on television. But I don't promote causes. People are in the eye and I have them on my show—it's what people expect."

"People like Darren Mackenzie—the suspected child abductor, people like him?" Macleod's face was deadly serious and showed a lot of contempt. "You allowed that pond life airtime. Everyone at the station said so."

"As I said people in the public eye. I don't book them; the team at the production company does. And the season on rights for gypsies was the same. And when I had Mr McKinney on."

"Mr McKinney, who is dead in the cave outside?"

"No, Pandie, over there. I didn't even know he had a partner until I got here. Well, I say that, but I knew he had a partner but I didn't know his partner, or anything about him. But Pandie is a strong advocator of LGBT rights, very strong in fact and in the public eye."

Macleod was quickly becoming aware that the public eye and he were not very well acquainted. He seemed to know very few figures that Miss Baxter talked about but he was beginning to form his suspicions on what was happening. An execution, a wholesale execution of certain figures. If someone had used Macaulay to build this elaborate trap, and it was ridiculously elaborate, that person would also need to have met him before.

161

"Your father, Miss Baxter, he was into this roleplaying. How far did he travel to do it?"

"All over. He'd disappear for long weekends, dressing up and running around castles and that. As I was growing up, he tried to get me involved. Nothing sinister, just role-play, knights and queens, monsters and demons, investigations into the strange. He had a thing for Lovecraft, M R James, horror and the like."

Again, the names washed over Macleod. "Did he spend his money on anything else?"

"Of course, but this roleplaying was where his heart was. Even when my mother had an affair at one she attended with him, he was not put off."

"When was that?"

"Five years ago. She dressed up as a shield maiden and got it on with a cleric. Not a real one, Inspector," said Miss Baxter as Macleod's face started. "They got caught doing it on the battlements and my father still went back to the same place the following year, though without her."

"A true role-player then," said Macleod.

"Although he could be a brilliant businessman, Inspector, he was always at home in these fantasy worlds. And it's gone and killed him." Miss Baxter bent over and sobbed. "He was so stupid with these damn made-up stories. There'll be no more of them now. He's scared me properly this time."

Macleod placed a distant but comforting arm on Miss Baxter. Normally he would not have been that forward during investigations but this one was different. He was rarely among the range of potential victims. When Miss Baxter had recovered to a degree where Macleod felt it was appropriate to leave her and move on to another of the guests, he stood up and sat down beside Mrs Johnston. The large-framed woman had red eyes from the tears she had shed for her husband and the stress of the situation was all over her face.

"I'm sorry to have to ask these questions I'm about to, but I need to know more about your husband. If he's alive I will need to move quickly to ensure he stays that way, so please be candid in all your responses." The woman nodded and sniffed.

"I understand the gravity of the situation, Inspector, more than most here, bar yourself and your colleague. Please, ask whatever you want."

"Why are you here?" The woman's face showed a lack of comprehension. "Why are you here?" repeated Macleod. "I mean, what links you to this place and Macaulay? Where did you meet him first? Did he actually invite you? Is this type of weekend, or rather the type of weekend it was meant to be, your cup of tea?"

"Oh, that's an easy one, Inspector. You see, my husband met Mr Macaulay some time ago, on a role-playing weekend. My husband has always been into these sorts of things. I think it was in England that they first met. I was not with my husband; indeed, we have only been together five years. We share a common love of the ancient, you see, although he is more steeped in the mythology. That is part of my studies too, but languages are where I truly find my feet. But the two complement each other well, like we do."

Macleod nodded. "And had he seen Macaulay since that first meeting?"

"Oh yes, they were common companions at these weekends. In fact, my husband was delighted when Mr Macaulay said he was going to run a weekend here in Scotland. Really, Jermaine, my husband's first name, Inspector, was so overjoyed he began to write to Mr Macaulay, giving him a plan of a potential story. I had to translate some language for him as well. I've seen some of it on the walls."

Yes, thought Macleod, *that explains a lot. The man was so keen when we first split into groups, even carrying on after his injury, shuffling his arse across a bloody floor while others nearly had a breakdown at the sight of it, all of those decapitated puppets.*

"Did he, or you, know any of the other guests here?" asked Macleod.

"No, but then that is not uncommon. Throwing people together was always one of the traits of these role-play games. I have only attended a couple but you have to then pull together, find out about each other. That's not always easy for me, Inspector. I'm quite aloof normally, being of such an academic bent, and men do not tend to flock to me like they would Miss Baxter or Miss Blayney. The brain is not valued so highly as these modern feminist movements would have you believe. Even us girls like a body attached to the sweet-talking mouth of a man."

"Yes, it's not right," agreed Macleod.

"I never said that, Inspector. Maybe nature is nature. That's what Jermaine would say. You should not subvert what is normal. Only that which is not."

"What did he mean by that?"

"I thought it was obvious, Inspector. Sorry, that was rather arrogant of me. You see, I can give off a rather superior disposition at times; it's not healthy for making friends. Jermaine always said we should be who we are and not what parties force us to be."

Macleod was intrigued, if feeling a little out of his depth. "Go on, please."

"I think one of them today is often referred to as the PC brigade. Political correctness, not being allowed to say what is on your mind, or even what is, because of damning indictment about what you have said rather than whether or not it's right."

"Did he have strong views himself, or was this just an observation on our way of life?"

"Oh, he railed against the establishment. Country to the dogs, academia being trumped. I found that hard at times as I'm quite a socialist, Inspector. At heart I could be a sixties' hippie. It caused some discord amongst us. Quite heated at times."

Macleod saw a touch of regret in the woman's eyes. "But you stayed together so it could not have been that bad."

"On the contrary, Inspector, it was bad enough that we stopped talking about real world issues; these role-play games, or any other sort of fantasy, was where our relationship lived."

"This may be a jump too far, Mrs Johnston, but you don't seem a woman who would settle for that."

"Indeed, I am not. But I am a woman of needs and as I already said, men don't come my way every day like they do for Miss Blayney or Miss Baxter. Please, Inspector, don't try and say different. And don't pretend that you have cast a glance at my figure as you have at Miss Baxter's or Miss Blayney's. It's normal. I enjoyed poor Mr McKinney's before his demise and Mr Brace's impressive form but have hardly given you a glance for your physical features. But mentally you do stimulate, but in a completely different way."

Macleod was unsure of whether he should feel insulted. His body was in good shape for his years. Jane liked it, did she not? And then the ego dropped away. *Yeah, she's right*, thought Macleod. *I might be with Jane because of her disposition, her*

165

kindness, her fun-loving ways but the first attraction was her body.
Actually, her hair. Mrs Johnston is right.

"Then the loss is their own," said Macleod.

"You're very kind, Inspector, but a very poor liar."

Chapter 19

There was a rattle on the car door and Hope woke with a start. She desperately looked around her until she realised that a shower of hail was beginning. Although wrapped up in a blanket, she was bare underneath and that frightened her. If Brace found the car and came at her, she would be exposed, for want of a better word.

Her hand wandered to the seat beside her and the steering wheel to find her clothes. They were still damp but not sodden anymore. She was not sure how warm they would be once on but for now the blanket was dry and she was warm in the car. Looking at the fuel gauge she realised that there was less than a quarter of a tank left. Then she realised she had no idea how long that meant if you were not driving the car. Her only experience with the fuel tank was on journeys, not when staying in the same spot.

The snow around the vehicle told Hope that she was unlikely to dig it out on her own, and even if she did the road was invisible under the snow. She could easily ditch the vehicle into another hole. No, the trek back would be done on foot. But just not yet.

Anders Larsen was dead. It was hard to take, she was a police officer, and it was her job to keep him alive. She had barely survived herself and she thanked her mother for the shouts and arguments on a Saturday morning that had driven her to the swimming pool. "You'll need it one day, you'll see," her mother had said. She was right, after all these years. It was a pity she was not around to be thanked.

What would Brace's plan be? Surely, he would be making his way back to the house. Hope looked beyond the windscreen and saw the hail being whipped around in circles and then blown this way and that. It looked brutal out there.

She wondered if Macleod would be any further on with the investigation. How could he be? Brace was out here. But why was Brace doing this? When McKinney had died there was always the homophobic angle. But Macaulay was not a homosexual. At least if he was, it was a damn good act the way he was all over Melanie Blayney. That girl could certainly keep a man's attention. But then maybe Macaulay was just in the way.

And why here for Brace? He was a guest, invited in. Or was he placed? Hope looked at the sea in the distance. If you wanted to kill someone and get away with it, what better way than to have a few *accidents*. Machinery fails and the man who made them is dead, too. That's a neat story. Maybe that was the angle. But would you be on your own?

No. Too much risk, best to have numbers, people who could influence. So who was invited, and who was initiating? The Chief Inspector had been invited; Macleod and she were just extras, substitutes. What had the big boss been doing to incur wrath? Diversity? The new diversity drive and policy push? She had also been the one instrumental in getting the conviction of abuse on the university in Glasgow who had been blocking female promotion to the professorships. Was this why she was targeted?

Would someone be angered enough to kill? Macleod was struggling with all these changes. Anything that's a bit unusual and he's struggling on the inside. But he's like a lot of struggling people, prepared to live and let live, prepared to let people have their lives, prepared to change, albeit slowly. But someone isn't. Or is it a group? To pull this off would require a team. Someone on the inside. Maybe the Smiths.

And from the outside, influence on Macaulay while this was built. Inside access to change it. This whole thing was elaborate. And who knew where it would stop? But they could not have planned the weather. Was some of it ad hoc? She thought of Brace's face when she had made her comment about possibly having had a relationship with another woman. He'd gone cold right there and then. Prior to that he'd been interested, despite having had an eighteen-year-old gymnast on his arm.

Another shower of hail hit the vehicle and Hope shivered. But as she looked outside, she knew there were only two options; sit here and leave Macleod to his own devices hoping that the DSC alarm had worked, or return to the house and help her boss out.

Survival, she had told him. He had no friends up there, no one he could really trust. Hope flung the blanket off her shoulders and shook as the cool air of the car made her skin goosebump. As she pulled on her underwear, she found it still damp and ignored the uncomfortable feeling as she dragged it over her skin. When she finally put her coat on, she sat for a few minutes more while the present hail shower passed.

Brace, I need to watch out for Brace so I should route overland, not up the coast, because he knows that way. She turned off the car engine and zipped her coat as far up as it could go. She was still cold, but less chilled. Opening the car door, she cursed as the wind bit into her cheek. She grabbed the blanket that had been her comfort for the last hours and began to wrap it around her, focusing on her exposed cheeks.

Hope started forward and spied a hump of ground in the distance. There was a sprig of heather sticking up and she made this her marker. Behind her, she saw the car and made sure to stay in a line between the two. There were no other markings, a perfect white tapestry. If there had been trees then she would have had a better vista to navigate but here there was little, so deep had the snow fallen. You didn't see this sort of thing in Glasgow, never mind Harris.

Sometimes she wished she was an American cop and could use a firearm. Brace was large, a superbly built athlete and Hope would struggle to apprehend him. With a firearm she could tag him. But then he would surely carry one if he thought she, or rather her kind, did.

The blanket became wet quickly and she thought about whether she should simply drop it and expose her face to the elements but at this time it was coping. As the sprig of heather approached she breathed a sigh and looked for her next marker. Her arms wrapped around her, she struggled on, her foot sinking every now and again as the undulating land beneath allowed the snow to break and fall down from its faint bridge. Footing could be at a premium in a fight. Maybe this could even the odds.

Hope had stayed clear of the shore but she was also unaware of what time it was or how long she had slept. Where would Brace be? And should she simply come to the door or would it be better to sneak up on the house and be a pair of watching

170

eyes from outside? Of course, by that she meant outside the party, not the building. She needed to get inside as soon as possible due to the cold. But how would she get in? There was a large hole in the roof, and there was the outside barn—maybe that had a way in. The building would surely be locked if they were trying to keep someone out or restrict movement.

Hope pulled the now-wet blanket around her and heard the ice falling from it. It was not quite a tingle of shards, more a drop of hail onto the ground but it confirmed what she knew. The blanket was sodden and freezing and becoming useless.

A new burst of snow was coming in and the smaller mountains in the distance were becoming obscured behind the grey clouds that were getting darker by the minute. The wind whipped up again and the squalls began, buffeting Hope as she walked. She was sure her cheeks were burning and found this such a weird sensation in the snow. But the house had just been in sight before the storm increased. Now it was gone and she could barely see 200 feet ahead.

And then she saw a shadow. Or was it something else. It was a figure. Hope dropped to the ground huddled in her blanket. The figure was less than a hundred metres away but was already nearly on the edge of her view. She didn't move and wrapped her head tighter into the blanket ensuring her red hair was covered. Lying as still as she could keep, she saw Brace, or at least a figure resembling his build walking through the storm ahead of her. Where had he been that he was still out here?

There was no time to think about that but instead she started after him, staying on the edge of visibility as the storm pressed. Her nose felt frozen and her feet were starting to lose sensation. But the fire inside Hope was burning bright as she saw her

171

target walking. A rage was building as she thought about Anders Larsen and Brace's cold dealing with them both.

Brace seemed to be walking to the rear of the house, as far as Hope could tell in the storm. She prayed for a relenting of the storm so she could see exactly where the large house was. It was during a moment of abatement that Hope had to dive into the ground and keep her head low as Brace looked around. When there was no cry or acknowledgement, Hope sneaked a look up and saw her target moving away, seemingly happy that all was well.

Her heart was beating fast and she thought about catching Brace and holding him in court for the judge to throw away the key. He had killed an innocent man and tried to kill her and now he was acting like he would return to the house to kill another guest.

The storm eventually passed by leaving a slow fall of snow against a light grey backdrop. The wind was strong but not so variable and the visibility had lifted a little bringing the house into view. But Brace was routing to the rear and a barn that was a little away from the house. He passed by it and then approached a small area that seemed to sink slightly into the ground. While the rest of the land had a rolling undulation, this seemed different, man-made and Hope wondered what he was up to.

And then the man disappeared. Hope had laid down again and as he looked about she had lowered her head to the ground. When she looked back up about a half minute later he was gone. She thought she had heard a slight tap, like something closing but compared to the wind it was so faint it made her unsure of her own senses.

She dropped the blanket and approached the area of mystery

quickly. As she arrived, Hope saw the double flaps that sat in the ground. Cautiously, she opened one side and stepped inside. There were descending steps and she delicately closed the door behind her. For a moment she just listened, Brace was moving up ahead and breathing heavily. When Hope believed there was distance between them, she stepped forward in the dark, her arms feeling for the walls. Slowly, carefully, she edged her way along.

She could no longer hear Brace and believed him to be far ahead now. He did not have to recce in the dark as she did. She edged around a corner and felt along the wall. Then she felt an arm or some vestige of skin and almost jumped. Fighting her emotions and desire to scream, Hope felt along the arm until she reached where the head would be. There was no head. Her heart thumped. And then the figure slumped onto her, knocking her over. There was a click. Every fibre in her body screamed at Hope to move.

Chapter 20

Hope threw her arms forward, pushing the body away from her and rolled as fast as she could to one side. Something caught her arm and she winced as behind her she could hear something whirring and slicing. As she lay on the floor, she saw a green glow from the wall and in the light there seemed to be a number of circles of teeth. A body, one which she presumed had been the one on top of her, was shredded and liquid was spraying here and there. And then the teeth and something dark hovered above the remains before engulfing them, like they had been eaten.

Hope tried to stop herself from panicking but she was shaking. Maybe it was a combination of the cold or the fact that death had looked at her again but she was unable to stop the involuntary movement. Part of her wanted to scream but she knew it would give her position away. Maybe someone would come to check, maybe not. Were these devices automated or was there someone looking on and causing the carnage?

As she lay on the ground, Hope became aware that her blouse was becoming sodden. She sniffed the liquid now rolling cross the floor. Blood possibly but not the blood she was used to. Animal maybe? Macleod had mentioned about the copious blood at the first scene he had gone to.

Getting up onto her knees, Hope's instincts took over and she remained quiet working her way along the opposite wall, praying that nothing was going to eject from there. Soon she reached a door and carefully pushed it. There was a storeroom, with basic sanitary products, chemical solutions and the like. A cleaner's cupboard. Hope stepped inside and shut the door behind her, pushing a mop up against it. She propped the other end against the wall jamming the door. And then she placed her head in her hands and shook violently crying into her palms.

"Bastard, bloody bastards," she muttered under her breath. The face of Anders Larsen came to mind. Again, she cried. It was not normal for police to be there at the murders; they usually picked up the pieces afterwards and jailed the bad guys. *Why am I fighting for my life*, she raged.

At the yoga class they taught you to breathe easy and she tried to bring back the practice she had given up after only four weeks. Her arms extended and she exhaled through her nose before sucking back in through her mouth. *That was it, nice and easy, keep it going, girl, just keep it going.*

Something moved in the room, causing the bucket to sound, and then came some faint scratching. Hope fought hard not to shriek and stood up quickly backing away from the bucket. What was coming now? Would she be attacked?

Looking into the bucket, she relaxed. A field mouse was running around inside and causing a ruckus. Hope almost laughed and then stared at the little fur ball with the tail. *Yes,* she thought, *that's us. Running around and around and getting nowhere. We'll all be dead if we keep doing this.*

Gathering herself together, Hope reminded herself she was the law here and if no one was present she would have to enforce it. Releasing the door and stepping back into the corridor, she cautiously continued along the passageway until it split. One way descended down some steps, a small green light giving the dimmest view of a set of stairs she had ever witnessed. The route ended in a closed door and she quickly made her way up to it.

There was no peep hole or any other way to see what was on the other side. Delicately, she turned the handle. The door was stiff but with an easy push it swung open. Stepping through, she found herself in a room, lit by firebrand, that had a large number of decapitated bodies and heads lying around the floor. They were not human but looked more like weird little dwarfs or elves. The floor was covered in blood but obviously not human blood—the colour was not right.

This must have been the scene Macleod attended. He had said it was gross and he was right. Hope heard a click behind her and turned around looking for the door. But she couldn't see it. It had gone. How could that happen? She probed the wall with her fingers and could barely find the tracing lines. But then she felt a catch, or at least what she thought might be. But others would not have been so lucky, struggling to find where the door even began. Having come through it she had that advantage.

Flicking the catch, the door opened again and Hope exited to the corridor. The steps lay ahead, or else she would have to retrace her steps back to the cold outdoors. Hope decided she was going to end this and walked directly to the steps.

They were made of stone and the dim green light made them passable but Hope still believed they would be treacherous. There seemed to be a dampness emanating from below and she carefully made her way down. As she descended so she was below the level of the corridor above, her feet began to slap on the wet steps. Her hand touched the wall and it was wet and she detected a musty scent. She stopped momentarily, worried she was missing any sounds of someone ahead but there was nothing beyond the occasional drip of water.

Hope shivered as she walked, feeling the cold of the underground passage. Perhaps this made its way back to the house, she surmised, but in reality, she did not know the direction she was walking in. Her blouse was still soaking from the animal blood and her trousers stuck to her as well. In fact, she was sure some of the blood had got into her hair. But it needed to be finished. Brace needed to be stopped.

Hope continued along the passage until it started to dry out. There was still a musty smell but now when she touched the wall, it was drier and the corridor felt warmer. She arrived at a set of stone steps and slowly climbed them until she saw the top of her climb. Here, she kept close to the wall where the green lighting seemed at its dimmest, wary of anyone coming along the passage ahead. On reaching the upper passage, she realised that it split shortly after the summit into three other passages.

If you set up an elaborate game as this, thought Hope, *then you would need to keep control and these passages would allow you to appear, or check, or even set up areas of the house your guests would think you wouldn't reach. I wonder how many parts of the house can be reached in this way.*

There was no indication on the walls, no signage like the rear parts of a theatre or theme park. She would have to just pick a way to go and follow it. *But if Brace came this way*, she thought, *maybe he's left footprints of some trace.* Kneeling, she pored over the floor but there was little to aid her thoughts. While both

Aldo Brace and she had walked through the wet corridor, it seemed their shoes had deposited most of the liquid on the drier steps and the passage floor immediately before them. She had no sense of direction, of how the passage fitted into the scheme of the house.

Let's go left! There was no reason to be this assertive but she had always liked left over right, just one of those stupid things in life you develop for no good reason at all. Stopping for a moment to listen if anyone was ahead of her in any of the corridors, she finally decided she was as safe as could be expected in the circumstances and walked along the corridor to the left.

The passage was a short one and ended in a small door, about half the size of a person. Unless Macaulay had stolen some munchkins from some mythical master, this would be a secreted door in a room and Hope lent against it, trying to judge if anyone was in the room ahead. There was only silence beyond and she fumbled in the dim light for a door handle. There was a knob about half way up the door and when she tried to twist it, there was no movement. But when she pulled across the door with it, the knob slid across and must have released an internal fixing as the door began to swing open.

She pulled it back slowly and then peered into the room beyond. The room was poorly lit but Hope was unsure if this was the darkness outside or the thickness of the curtains at the window. Rather than alert anyone to her presence, she shut the small door behind her and stood in one spot examining the room.

The door behind her was subtly incorporated into a wall of certificates and paintings. There were men in smart garments, chains around their necks and colourful sashes across their chests. They were all looking serious but noble, and gave Hope the idea of a masonic lodge. However, she was familiar with some of the more common masonic symbols and markings and none of these matched. The men were also of a myriad of races. There were black men, ranging from light brown to the extremely dark skin of those born close to the equator. Others were Arab in visage, some oriental, and quite a few were European.

On another wall was a flaming sword with a gate behind it, writing underneath that seemed to be Latin although Hope could not translate it. She had a few bits of French, German, and even Spanish, garnered from investigating tourists during her short career on the force but Latin was not a subject she had tried at school. In fact, English had been bad enough without learning some dead language.

The room had only one desk which was one of those modern computer desks, narrow and made of metal with a screen on the top and a keyboard that slid out from underneath. Wires ran along the back and Hope noticed the camera perched onto the screen. A four wheeled office chair was before the desk. Otherwise there was no furniture.

The camera was currently pointing to the middle of the room and Hope stepped forward to become central and slowly rotated, taking in all four walls before her. There was the massive sword and gate motif on one, the pictures hanging on another, a third was taken up with the curtained window, and the last seemed to hold tapestries and framed pieces of paper. As secret societies went, this seemed to be a large one.

As she spun round, Hope realised why the camera was pointing at the centre of the room. She could almost feel the grandeur and pride soaking through someone looking up at the sword and gate motif, part of something bigger. In this connected world, maybe this was how a secret society ran, joining together across the internet and reciting . . .

What would they be reciting? That was the key to it. Macaulay had obviously been a man steeped in a fantasy life, an enjoyer of role-play and in itself there was little wrong with that. But what if the role-play was based on something darker. She had no idea who any of the people on the wall were, none were public figures, at least none from her world. If she had her mobile she would be photographing them all, sending it back to Glasgow and asking for some identifications to be made.

Hope stepped forward to read some of the framed papers on the wall. As she scanned them, she saw Macaulay's name on most of them and they seemed to be recorded rites of passage as he was being elevated in the organisation. This made Hope think that this was not a secret organisation that was operating deep under the radar, like a government secret service. This was more like a lodge but it seemed to be worldwide. What was the purpose of it? She ran her eyes over the collected framed items but came up with only one thing that said more than a simple congratulations of Macaulay's achievements.

On a piece of parchment, written on in red, there was a short but simple statement. It was written in Latin but underneath in a rather comic gesture was a piece of handwritten English. But Hope did not laugh.

When Man has been forsaken and cast to the cold,

We shall rise to protect and new life enfold,

In patterns of justice and a new Man to mould,

That will endure and last, until Paradise stand once more.

There was a hasty scribble underneath which said *couldn't get the last piece to rhyme.* Hope read between the flowery language, read the underlying implication of the words. Someone would make the world as they saw it. There was no democracy in the statement and if it is said in the dark then that surely is where the power is wielded from.

But she had no proof of any wrongdoing, just the words of boys-at-play. Except this weekend said different. Read with this context behind it, the weekend seemed like a premeditated murder session. But Macaulay was also dead. Was there a spat? Or was he just a boy who suddenly found his role-play was actually real play? Hope did not know but she knew there was something more sinister here than she had previously believed.

Then the computer suddenly beeped into life and Hope saw the screen come on. She pinned herself to the wall and then slid around to the curtains, placing herself behind them. The computer began to whir and she heard voices announcing themselves to some group. But the names were just animals and standings. *Elk Alpha, Cobra Beta, Coyote Delta.* The voices were intense. There was an impatience and although nothing else was said, it was like they were waiting for someone.

Hope thought she heard someone moving and then realised the small door was being opened. From behind the curtains it was hard to see. They were not opaque but they were too thick to see with any definition. But then a strong figure emerged from the small half door and walked to the centre of the room before bowing before the motif on the wall. He then turned to the computer and stood almost soldier-like. It was Brace.

Chapter 21

Hope stood completely still behind the curtain watching Brace check-in with other members of this secret organisation. It was not always clear but he certainly said something with his hand pressed to his breast, some sort of swearing in or promise. He was mostly silent after that until addressed. Hope's issue was that she could hear Brace well enough but the other men on the screen were quiet and she would rather have been closer to the computer speakers which were not pointed at her.

"The storm continues and we are still not disturbed so we will continue with the extension to the plan. There has been a few near misses but the remaining targets are now down to four," said Brace as he was asked for a report. He was quite comfortable as he spoke, his voice giving no hint of the deadly actions he had taken.

Hope did not hear the reply as the sound was tinny and quiet, but Brace responded. "We may have a day; the storm is due to abate soon. The problem is that the policeman may get more involved. With the death of our host, the plan has been somewhat adjusted. I believe we need to kill all four remaining targets."

Again, the computer screen flickered as someone spoke back

before Brace replied. "Very well, I shall report back in three hours. By then it will be complete. It will seem like a massive mechanical failure that killed them all, including Macaulay. Two will be missing presumed dead, having tried to get help in the boat." There was a grunt and a swing of his arm to his chest and Brace stepped forward to the computer and pressed a button. Turning on his heel, he exited the room.

Hope let the tension go from her body but waited behind the curtain. Her breathing was racing at the realisation Brace was now going to kill her boss and at least three others. But that meant not everyone was a victim; some were clearly in on this act. But who?

Macleod would be a victim, like she was meant to be. And then there was Pandie. With his partner having been eliminated, then Pandie must be a target. Was it their lifestyle that was offensive enough to have them murdered? What about the Johnstons? Sure, he was a moaning ass and she was a boring clever clogs but was there anything about them to make them a target? Zara Dawson? Was she in this with Brace? She was very young to be caught up but then, it had happened before, especially if she was into Brace. And what about Melanie Blayney? She came with Macaulay but he died. Would she be eliminated too in case she knew something? And what about the staff?

Hope knew she had to act, but what to do and how, she was unsure of. Stepping out from behind the curtain, she approached the computer and tried to turn it on, pressing the button Brace had used in switching it off. How were they getting a connection, she thought? The mobile signal was non-existent and telephone lines were not working. Maybe a satellite connection. Expensive but it would work.

The screen lit up but merely showed a space with the legend above it, *Password*. Dammit, thought Hope. She checked the rear of the computer but found no modem or phone connection, instead a wire disappeared into the wall.

Maybe Brace was returning to the group but he might also operate in the dark, allowing himself to strike the remaining targets more easily. She needed to get to Macleod and prevent these killings. But she was stuck on the wrong side of the house's elaborate maze of secret passages. She needed to get out. Hope opened the curtains and saw the day had nearly faded. Looking out onto the grounds at the front of the house she saw no one. There were no handles or other fixtures on the window that allowed it to be opened. She would have to use the passage she had come in from.

Carefully Hope opened the door and returned to the passage-way outside. She retraced her steps and took an unexplored passage. If she could not get anywhere using these passages, she would return via the long underground corridor to the outside and then come to the house by the front door. That would be a long walk and she hoped that this fast search of the surrounding passages would yield quicker results.

Taking a new corridor, Hope followed it left and then right before it ended in a door. She listened at it for a few moments, trying to ascertain if anyone was on the other side. She could not hear anything and so tentatively pushed the door open. Inside was a small room with a table, a kettle and a fridge. There were used cups on the table and she saw a small sink attached to the wall. Despite still being chilled, Hope resisted the temptation to make herself a hot drink and instead her eyes were drawn to the opening on the other side of the room. She tiptoed across and looked inside.

Her breath was almost taken away by the machinery in the room. There was a constant whir of air conditioning and several screens in front of a chair. A keyboard and a mouse also lay before the screens. Her eyes widened as she saw figures on the screen. There was Macleod, sitting at a table talking to Miss Baxter. She scanned the screen for the rest of the party and despite the slightly blurred quality of the image, she identified Pandie, Mrs Johnston, Miss Blayney, and the two staff. Where was Mr Johnston? Was he dead?

The group seemed to be calm if not in good spirits and she wondered what they were doing. They were definitely in the kitchen but did not seem to be on the move. Hope examined the rest of the screens. There were other rooms displayed, some of which she had not been in. Using the mouse, she clicked on various arrows on the screen and the view changed from one room to another, or an outside corridor. There was an image of the pier where she had been grabbed. She clicked on it and an image of Peter McKinney, still stuck on the cruel device that had killed him, flashed in front of her. She had seen death many times but Hope still felt sick looking at it. And yet this was distilled.

If you were there, you would smell his body, the beginning of decay. The dampness of the cave would make your skin crawl and the overlying weight of despair at the senselessness of death would kick at your mind. But here it was an image on a screen, and only the knowledge that it had been real kept Hope from simply glancing past it like she did on the television at home.

Was there some way she could shut down the devices? Hope could use a normal computer but she was no expert, merely a good user of the software. Looking at another screen, she saw what look like an operating interface. But there were no handy identifiers like, *flying monster that comes in through the window*. Instead she saw AD34, BD86, and SS23. None of these made any sense and neither was there any help from the other screens for these identifiers.

There were other identifiers like *armed*, *safety, fired* and *frozen*. Apart from the obvious, Hope was unsure just what these buttons would do to whatever device they were attached to. There also seemed to be a multitude of options that led off this interface and Hope was frankly lost.

She looked around behind her and saw several open racks that were blinking and occasionally whirring. These were obviously the hardware running the software but again it was all coded and nothing seemed to say what it was or what it did. But then Hope saw what looked like a rack of fuses with the little levers that could switch them off or on. Maybe she could simply switch these all off. But would that just alert Brace to her presence when nothing worked. She was aware that she was operating with privilege at the moment in that she was considered dead. Strange how that was a good thing.

Looking back up at the screen, she saw that the party in the kitchen were on the move, every single one of them. *What are you doing with them*, thought Hope, *surely it would be safer to stay put.* She watched the party leave the kitchen and then make their way into the library. As they entered with a ladder, Hope was aware of someone entering the door into the small kitchen beside the room she was in. She dove for the corner where she had seen the fuses. Squeezing herself behind the fuse rack she found herself having to breathe in tight. There were enough racks between her and the main desk so that if any glanced over she would be hard to see. If they had a proper look . . .

"I told you not to bring your wife; that's how we get into these situations." The voice was that of Aldo Brace.

"We were meant to only have one accident and that was meant to be after two days, and we would have had a perfect getaway. A simple accident but you had to push the agenda, pile up the bodies and now it's a damn mess." Hope saw Mr Johnston enter the room in a state of fluster and clearly angry at Brace.

"No wives. Macaulay brought a tart. I brought the silly gymnast bitch and all you had to do was bring someone else. Some tart with big tits that would keep you happy for the weekend and someone we could ditch if the shit hit the fan. Well, it's hit now and we need to be sure we are safe and clear by getting rid of the others. If your wife doesn't join up then she's for it too."

Brace sat down in the chair after these words and shook his head. But Johnston raged.

"Don't lecture me, sunshine. You haven't got the brains for this operation. Who put this all together, got Macaulay to outlay for it and make sure he wasn't none-the-wiser about it. He'd have been up to his neck with the Health and Safety Executive and we would be swanning off quite happily but now we will be up to our necks in blood. And we'll have to do the talking when the police show. Wasn't one gay enough for you? And what was the thing with the policewoman? You didn't need to take her out either."

"She was one of them," spat Brace. "God intended a body like hers for a man."

"When did she say she was a lesbian?" asked Johnston.

"She indicated it. Beside she's one of the crowd who

encourage them. Tolerance, diversity, and all that shit."

"You are obsessed," cried Johnston. "We didn't need to kill everyone. The point would have been made."

"Would it? How? An accident, a bloody accident, how does that make a statement? We should hang them from the balcony and tell the world."

"I don't care anymore," said Johnston. "Just leave Chrissy alone. She's not to be harmed."

"If she doesn't get out of the way then it's her own fault. In fact, it's your fault for bringing her. You needed a Barbie doll like me. Have some fun and toss her away. Little whore." Brace sat back and stared at the screens. "Anyway, look, they are on the move; that's perfect. I'll steer them to the ballroom—finish them all in there."

"Don't you do a thing until I get Chrissy out. You hear me Brace. I'll have you thrown out. You'll be nothing in the organisation."

"Don't count on it," sneered Brace. "Who do you think got the go ahead for this? Why did I get Macaulay to show his allegiance? The top table wanted him dead. Dead or joined up fully, not the fantasy society he thought he was in. He got what he deserved. Letting his daughter spread lies on the television like that. Man needs to sort out his own family."

"Do nothing until I'm back. You hear me, Brace. Nothing."

With that, Johnston left the room, his leg seeming to be working normally. Hope watched the screen and saw Macleod climbing a ladder to the ceiling of the library. And then a gas started to fill the screen.

"Good man," said Brace. "Back down, back along the path to the final room. Yes, Maddy, you tell them where to go, tell them good. Got a hell of a room for you, Inspector. You'll die like that bitch you brought."

Hope felt the anger rising and fought to control it. She wanted to simply knock the fuse rack to the floor, jump over it and throttle the life out of Brace. But there were at least three killers on the loose. Brace, Johnston and now, Maddy, Madeline Smith. She needed to think how to end this, and end it fast. But she was only a few feet from Brace and squashed up behind the electronic equipment. She'd need to surprise him because he was strong and fast. She stood and ran ideas in her head. But half an eye saw Macleod on the screens. He was walking into a trap and had no idea.

Chapter 22

"I think it's time to move out," said Macleod, looking over the rag tag bunch sitting in the kitchen.

"And we'll all come," said Miss Baxter. "I don't want to be left back here when you go. Inspector, I don't think any of us do with what you have discovered. Safety in numbers. That's what you said at first. So we all go."

Macleod looked around at the remaining guests who seemed to be nodding their ascent. "Very well. Mr Smith, kindly remain at the rear of our party and those who think they may struggle physically please keep to the middle."

Macleod saw Miss Blayney rise to her feet and make for the front. "Do you think that's wise after your incident? You still look groggy."

Melanie Blayney smiled. "Your wingman is still not back and you need someone a bit more agile than yourself with you. I'm all right, and besides, if I'm going to die in this place, I'm going down fighting."

Macleod let Miss Blayney to the front and then asked everyone to move out, back to the library. Walking back into the book-laden room, Macleod found it eerily quiet and was half-expecting something to come back out of the large hole in the ceiling.

190

"There's a bit of a climb and then a crawl for everyone to do as we reach the tunnel to Macaulay's office. Please stay close." With that Macleod stood on the first rung of the ladder and then began to ascend to the floor above. As he made his way he heard a hiss from above.

"Inspector!" shouted Mrs Johnston.

Macleod looked up and a green gas was emerging from the room above and starting to descend into the library.

"What is it?" shouted Miss Baxter.

"Down, Seoras, get down. That could be anything," said Miss Blayney in a stern voice.

Macleod began to climb back down the ladder and then began waving everyone out of the room. Once they had all exited, he closed the door on the room and pondered his next move. He asked Mr Smith to come up to the front of the party.

"Do you know what's closest to the office I found? What room would be beside it? Maybe there's another way into these secret passages."

"Do you still have the map you found?" asked Smith and Macleod produced it. The drawings were very basic in outline but there was a general order to the design. The issue was that only the secret passages were shown with exit points and they were labelled with simple codes, such as DT10, all of which meant nothing to Macleod.

"You need to give me a rough idea of the distances you came," said Smith as his mother approached Macleod.

"Can I be of help?" she said. "I know this house as well as my son does. Maybe two heads will be better."

Macleod nodded and then recounted his journey and how long he thought the secret passages were. He had Miss Blayney come forward and give her impression too. After some consideration, the Smiths disagreed.

"The ballroom would be the best option," said Mrs Smith. "From what you've said, Inspector, I believe you were probably on the opposite side of the wall with the fireplace."

"I don't see that," said Kyle Smith. "It's further along, closer to the billiards room. That's where I would go."

"Kyle," said his mother, "you are getting confused. You weren't here for a lot of the transformation. I was."

"I thought you were both sent away," said Macleod.

"We were," said Mr Smith, "but mother was requested to return a few times to make sure Mr Macaulay had enough supplies and that. I was on a food course at the time, making use of the downtime, I suppose, although the boss did pay for it."

"And you think you saw something then that puts this room closer to the ballroom, Mrs Smith? Could she be right, Kyle?" asked Macleod.

"Maybe." But Macleod thought he sounded unsure.

"Okay, we'll go the ballroom first and then on to the billiards room if we find nothing. But stay close together, these are both new rooms and by what you are saying, Mrs Smith, there may be some of these monster animations in these rooms. I don't want to lose anyone else."

The party routed to the stairs before climbing them and then following a corridor, Mrs Smith leading the way. Macleod was finding it difficult to distinguish one corridor from another as they were all a mass of paintings and similar formal wallpaper. But after turning this way and that, they arrived at a large wooden door which Mrs Smith indicated as the destination.

"I'll go in first," said Macleod, "and when you follow, stick together."

Miss Blayney strode forward beside Macleod and put her hand on the door. "I'll go in first," she said. "We can't have our main investigator falling to a simple trap." Macleod went to argue but she flicked her hair and smiled at him. For a moment, he thought how impressive she was but then caught himself, focusing back on the room at hand.

The room was grand in the extreme. The walls were wooden panelled and had many pictures and drapes hung around them. Getting closer to the pictures, Macleod saw an image of what he thought must be a ghoul. Then he saw the body on the ground and the piece of flesh in the ghoul's hand. His heart jumped, not from the picture but because any room like this was part of the game and that meant a trap was more than likely. And they were all now inside.

"I suggest we stay close to the doors so we can escape quickly should anything happen," said Macleod.

Miss Dawson was clearly shaken by this statement and made for the door. As she approached it, the opening shut tight with a dramatic slam. She grabbed the handle and pulled but the door did not budge. Kyle Smith then grabbed the handle but he could make no headway with the door either. As he kept pulling, he suddenly screamed before releasing his hands, desperately blowing on them.

"It was hot," he shouted, "the bloody handle got hot."

Miss Dawson screamed and began crying out, shouting at some invisible person, calling them sick and twisted. She was reaching hysterical levels when a slap from Mrs Johnston stopped her abruptly.

"Calm down, girl. That will not help. We need another exit, I believe, Mr Smith." Despite having lost her husband, the woman was a solid rock in the party and Macleod was impressed by her coolness under what must be a frightening and devastating situation. Her husband was probably dead, at least in her eyes. Macleod had his suspicions but she would not see it the same way.

The wooden floor on which they stood began to shake and then split apart in the middle of the floor, creeping slowly back to either wall. It simply disappeared into the wall and revealed a white base underneath. Macleod grabbed Miss Blayney's arm as she stood next to him.

"Get over to wherever Mrs Smith goes."

"Why?" asked Miss Blayney.

"Just do it."

The party were standing on the wooden part of the floor but as it retreated into the wall at either end, they were forced to stand on the white base underneath. It was like ice, slippery and provided no traction. Mrs Johnston was the first to fall over going down with a sickening thump. Macleod shouted for everyone to grab hold of something and Miss Baxter grabbed Macleod's arm, dragging him down and then his feet went from under him. Miss Baxter fell on top of him and he fought to get her off of him and return to his feet.

Just as everyone seemed to be at least righting themselves into a seated position, the lights in the room went out. Miss Dawson screamed and Macleod saw the far end of the room where the fireplace had stood was now becoming a swirling vortex. It was similar to what had been seen before in other rooms, part of the overall theme of the weekend, no doubt. But Macleod was aware that there may be an added deadly element and he waited for something to emerge from the vortex, or for something to strike him from out of the dark.

The vortex was a swirl of lights, incredibly convincing, and the air became cold, a draught blowing across the scrabbling guests. And then the floor began to tip up, the fireplace end being the fixed point and the other end rising. Macleod was in the middle of the floor with Miss Baxter and they began to slowly slide along.

How the other guests were managing was unclear except that Miss Dawson was constantly screaming. Macleod tried to find a hold on the floor, anywhere. But there was none and Miss Baxter simply clung to him restricting his efforts to move elsewhere.

"Has anyone got a grip on anything? Anyone else not moving?" shouted Macleod, above the roar of the wind that was racing through the ballroom.

"Mrs Smith has a grip. And I have her," shouted Miss Blayney.

Macleod could not see where Miss Blayney was but he knew the voice was on his left. "Reach out, both of you. Everyone try to grab hold of them."

Macleod pushed Miss Baxter off him and she screamed, realising she was on her own. They were moving quicker now and racing right towards the swirling vortex. The light from the constructed illusion allowed him to see there was a drop beyond it, right in the centre of the fireplace. Looking as closely as he could, Macleod could see someone ahead of him. The figure was slight, and moving rapidly, screaming as it raced to the drop. Then it reached up and threw itself up and seemed to catch hold of something.

It had to be Zara Dawson, petite but with the muscles of a gymnast to hold herself up on whatever she had found above the vortex. Macleod prayed she would look back to himself and hopefully would extend an arm.

There were dull thuds as others hit the wall rather than shoot into the gap at the fireplace. But Macleod was heading straight for the drop

"Zara, give me your hand, now!"

Macleod raced under the gymnast and felt himself start to drop but he was held by a strong hand. Looking up he saw her hanging upside down and grimacing as she held him. He grinned his relief until an arm grabbed his leg and pulled at him. Miss Baxter was clinging onto him for her life as the three of them dangled together, Zara Dawson fighting hard to hold on.

As he hung there, Macleod heard a scream and then a curse that he swore came from Mrs Smith. Beside him, he saw a figure race into the drop and scream briefly before he heard a dull slap of a body into water.

"Got you," came a cry and Macleod struggled to know who had grabbed who. "No! Chrissy!" There more yells and shouts in the dark before the lights came on abruptly. The floor began to re-emerge and Macleod caught a quick glimpse of the drop below him before it was covered up. There was a body floating down below but he could not see who it was.

As soon as the floor was below her, Zara Dawson dropped Macleod who fell on top of Miss Baxter who either had been knocked out or had fainted from the effort. The young gymnast spun and dropped down beside Macleod in a move he could only dream of.

Looking around, Macleod started counting guests. *Seven? How could there be seven? Who fell through?* Then he saw Mr Johnston trying to grab his wife and encouraging her to leave.

"We have to go, Chrissy. It's okay, we can get away. You can't stay here with these people. They have to die but you don't.

It's all gone wrong; we need to go."

Macleod tried to stand up but he struggled and fell back to the floor again. Johnston was pulling at his wife but she was resisting. "We need to help them, Jermaine. What do you mean, have to die? This is no role-play. This is serious."

"Come on, Chrissy," said Johnston, dragging her to her feet. "It's all over; go!"

Something hit Johnston on his side and he tumbled to the floor. As he rolled over, Macleod saw Melanie Blayney getting off the floor above Johnston. "I have him, Inspector!"

Macleod took his time and managed to stand. As he looked around, he saw injuries all around him. But of the seven guests he had entered the room with, six were still alive. That was a good count. But Kyle Smith was hobbling to the fireplace. "Mum? Mum!"

"She pushed me out onto the floor," said Miss Blayney. "She tried to shove me to the lights but I was ready and held her so we spun around. She went straight in."

Macleod saw Kyle Smiths face begin to rage. "You killed her. You bloody killed her." He ran over to Melanie Blayney and threw her a punch to her jaw, causing the woman to fall backwards and Macleod thought she had gone out cold from the attack. Macleod ran over to Smith and grabbed his arm thrusting it up behind him, but the man was already dropping to his knees, sobbing bitterly.

Macleod followed him to the floor and held his arm tight until he was sure Smith was no longer resisting. As he searched the faces of those around him, he saw Pandie holding his arm like it was broken, Miss Baxter and Miss Blayney both out cold, and Christine Johnston being comforted by Zara Dawson. But where was Mr Johnston?

197

The door of the room shut hard and Macleod shouted back to Pandie as he ran across the room. "Look after them, and I'll get help when I've caught Johnston. Flinging open the door, he heard Christine Johnston wailing but he was undeterred. He had seen a killer and he would have his man.

Chapter 23

From her position behind the electrical racking, Hope could see the screens and watched as Macleod and his party entered a new room. It seemed large from the screen and she saw Brace becoming excited. His fingers hovered over the small mouse which drove the on-screen cursor.

"That's it," said Brace out loud to no one. "'This one is good, Inspector, might even get all of you with this one. Now get to the side, Maddy, and we'll get this show on the road." He gave a mean chuckle and Hope began to sweat. She needed to work fast but had got herself stuck behind the rack. Breathing in, she tried to slide out but with the proximity of her to the racking she was worried she'd rattle it and give herself up in an exposed position.

"In fact," continued Brace, "let's have you as the first victim, Zara. Stupid little child that you are, wouldn't know what a man wants. Laugh at me in the shower, you'll pay for that." Brace clicked the mouse and Hope saw the screen go dark. Swirling lights came on and as she watched the scene unfold, she heard screams, piped through to this small control room. There was no time; she needed to act.

Raising her hands from her sides up to above her head, she

pushed the racking forward, causing it to tumble and land on the back of Brace's head. But the bottom of it slid backwards and trapped her foot, jamming it against the wall. Brace swore and tried to extract himself from the racking lying on him. Equipment fell to the floor, smashing and causing sharp shards to race across the floor. As Brace pushed the racking off his head, he managed to turn around in his chair.

"You! Where did you come from? I killed you—that boat should have sunk in that weather."

Hope grimaced at the pain in her leg but she was determined to show Brace an angry face. "You are under arrest for the murder of Anders Larsen and any other dead body in this house I can pin on you."

"I ain't going down for no lesbian bitch." Brace shoved the racking and it swung back at Hope who flung her hands up as it bounced back into her. Her foot was freed up but Brace had his hands through the racking before she could react, grabbing her by the throat. She choked and put her own hands on his head. As he shook her, she fought for purchase and when her hands slid off his hair, she drove both thumbs into his eyes.

Brace yelled and his grip released. But he pushed the racking as he turned away, making it clatter off Hope again, cutting her forehead. Realising he was momentarily stunned, she stepped out to the side of the racking as he blinked his eyes which she prayed would be obscured to some degree. But within seconds he was back at the ready to attack again. Hope was now free of the racking but he had her pinned in a corner and she would have to fight her way out. It was the very situation she had wanted to avoid.

Brace reached forward and managed to grab Hope's shoulder, pushing her back against the wall and driving her head off it. She was temporarily shaken and barely saw the fist driving towards her. She leaned away but it caught her shoulder, and pain ripped through her body. She reached forward bringing Brace into a clinch. Her ear was bitten into and she fought hard to control her actions. She grabbed his shoulders and drove a knee hard up into his groin. And then did it again and again. His hands released and he started to stumble backwards. Hope swung a fist but missed wildly and then sucked in as much air as possible.

The screams from the room were still coming from the speakers and Hope registered that she needed to help. Brace was rolling on the floor and she tried to step past him but he grabbed her leg. She drove the other into his face and then reached for the mouse. She looked at the screen and saw where Brace had clicked earlier. The word "Disarm" was highlighted red and she clicked on it before looking at the screen to see if any change would take place. Lights came on in the room and she saw numerous figures congregated at the end nearest a fireplace. Macleod was there. He was all right, he was . . .

She felt the hands on her back and quickly placed her hands before her as she was driven towards the console. Her head hit but at a much-reduced force and she was able to then reach round with a hand to grab Brace's face. She found an ear and yanked it hard which released the weight of him on her as he stood up. She slipped clear and grabbed the mouse off the console desk.

"I'll kill you, you bitch," yelled Brace. "No slut is going to stop me!"

But Hope was now nearest the kitchen and had the mouse in her hand. She waved it in front of Brace and prayed he would take the bait. He stepped forward and she ran out of the door into the kitchen area and then out to the corridor.

Now she was clear of the tight confines of the control room and kitchen, Hope realised she did not have a plan. She was merely acting as bait, something to draw Brace away from his screens. But she had no idea where she was drawing him to. If she repeated her steps, came back the way she had followed to get to this point it would mean long corridors and Brace would probably catch up with her. She reached the junction that had led to the control room and took the one path she had not previously followed.

The echoes of Brace's footsteps rebounded along the corridor and as she ran along she wondered what she would do if this passage came to a dead end. But then again, why would it? There must be something here. As she rounded a corner she got her answer. In front of her was a door. It was small, about half the height and width of a standard door but nonetheless somewhere to keep running. Fumbling for a catch with which to open the door, Hope found it quickly, slid back a bolt and then pushed the door open. The interior was dark and Hope hesitated. Then she heard a cry.

"There you are, you bitch!"

Plunging herself through the reduced door, Hope's eyes struggled to adjust and she waved her hands about in front of her to try and find anything that would impede her progress. From the clip of her feet on the floor, she realised it was wooden and she was making easily traceable noises on it. Sliding onto her bottom, Hope reached down and removed her shoes. She could see the silhouette of Brace coming through the door, the corridor lights the only penetration of light in the room. Quietly, she crept into the far corner of the room, her hands gently searching her surroundings for a weapon. But none was forthcoming and now she felt trapped, wondering how to deal with the raging killer before her.

****

Macleod tore along a corridor that he did not recognise from his previous travels around the house and spotted Johnston up ahead. The injury to his knee had been a fake and the man seemed to be able to make as good a speed around these tight areas as Macleod. With every twist and turn, Macleod was puffing hard, his days of youthful and spritely pursuit behind him.

Johnston turned around a corner ahead of Macleod and the detective ran as hard as he could so as not to lose sight of the man for long. As he rounded the corner, something copper and the size of a small football was right in his path, at head height and he threw up his hands in vain. The bedpan caught him square in the face and Macleod's feet continued the journey whilst the rest of him stopped, causing him to fall backwards onto the floor.

Before Macleod could react, Johnston was on top of him, throwing a punch into Macleod's face. It struck without any great force but Macleod could not move as Johnston was on top of him and the man's bulk was enough to pin Macleod. Hands fumbled, trying to get past Macleod's arms which were waving in front of his face, fighting desperately to stop Johnston getting any sort of hold on his face. And then he felt them being separated.

Johnston pushed Macleod's arms back and then freed one of his own hands, looking to punch down hard but this left Johnston's face only a matter of some twelve inches from Macleod's face. He had been in too many fights over his career to hesitate. With everything he could muster, Macleod threw his head forward, smashing his forehead into Johnston's nose. There was a sickening crunch and the man screamed allowing Macleod to roll to the side, tipping Johnston off him in the process.

Once clear, Macleod saw his opponent rolling in agony, hands across his face. The detective scrambled over on his knees and sought to simply grab the prone man's arm and drive it up behind his back and secure him. As he made for the arm, Macleod saw that the pain Johnston was showing was a disguise as an elbow came up to meet him and caught Macleod just below the eye. He fell backwards. The blow was not strong and he saw Johnston take to his feet and start to run again.

Macleod stood up and began to pursue, nearly tripping on the bedpan lying on the floor. His eyes briefly saw the hooks that were the only fixtures in place where the bedpan should have been on the wall. With a shake of the head, Macleod set about his task again. The man had turned left up ahead. As he reached the corner, Macleod moved on a wide berth and saw a short but empty corridor ahead. Approaching slowly, he saw it ended in a large bureau over which was a portrait of Macaulay looking in a more jovial mood than he did after his decent from the balcony. The side of the corridor also had some pictures but Macleod could neither see nor feel any false doors.

But the man had gone somewhere. Macleod checked the floor but again there was nothing. Looking above, the ceiling gave no clues. There was no light to pull down on for a stepladder to somewhere. There was nowhere to go except . . . Macleod looked at the bureau and then at the floor directly underneath it. He could not see far under it but he noticed that the dust had gathered under the furniture. Except in the middle of the item there was no dust, only at the exterior edges.

Macleod grabbed the bottom of the bureau. He found to be flimsy and it flew upwards rotating as it did so, disappearing into the bureau leaving a space a man on his knees could shuffle through to a hole in the wall behind. Macleod did not hesitate but got down on his knees and shuffled his way through the hole in the wall. Beyond was darkness, but his man must have gone through here.

Chapter 24

Hope fought to control the terror inside at being trapped in the dark room with the large, more powerful, and murdering Aldo Brace. He had tried to kill her once already and the memory of her time in the cold water and then the scramble to a stuck car only added to the fear she was feeling. She was telling herself to think, telling herself to relax and be calm, breathe easy and steady. But the reality was too much and she felt hollow inside.

Brace was not giving much away since he entered the room and this comforted her. It meant he realised she was no pushover and she'd already dealt him a few strong blows which would be smarting. Normally, she felt comfortable tackling most people but Brace was an athlete, one used to hard collisions, and someone had taught him a little about fighting—of that Hope was sure.

Her hands continued to explore the area around her, her eyes being useless in the dark. Unlike most other places she had been in the house, this really was a dark room, a place with no exterior light or electrical sources providing a beacon on the blackness. Her hand touched something but she realised quickly that it was large and heavy, possibly the leg of a bureau or table. She could do with a knife or a bludgeon, something to keep him at a distance if he came for her, or to knock him out with from behind. Or a knife to kill with if it came to that. After all this was survival.

A noise came from the wall furthest from Hope and she saw something open and light suddenly stream in, blinding her temporarily. The opening shut again quickly and Hope heard footsteps as someone seemed to stumble in the room.

"Who's that?" shouted Brace.

"You! You tried to kill her, you ignoramus. I told you not to do anything until I had her." It was Johnston's voice.

"That was your fault; you brought her. You knew everyone else was expendable. All you had to do was bring a stand-in."

"You've never been married. You don't know what questions would have been raised. And why are you here? Who's in the control room?" asked Johnston.

"She's in here. The Inspector's bitch. Doesn't go down easily."

"Where?" cried Johnston, panicking. "I have Macleod on my tail. I just lost him. We need to go."

"Go where, you fool. Don't you realise it's all gone to pot. We need to get rid of them all. I need to dispose of this cop and her boss. And then we need to eliminate the rest. Make it a horrific accident. Your precious wife too, if she doesn't get with it."

"You leave Chrissy alone!"

Hope used the bickering to slide away from the voices, looking for something else in the room she could use. But the sheer darkness meant she was struggling to find anything and then identify it. But Macleod was nearby; that at least was something. He had survived the ballroom episode. But if he came into the room the same way Johnston had, he would be

207

exposed and probably unsure of his surroundings, open to be attacked. She would need to be ready.

"If you were in the control room, you could just lock the doors in here and gas them. We can operate everything from there. Finish everyone off from there and then get away," shouted Johnston.

"Get away? That would bring questions. No, we need to have an accident, have the house collapsing. Or maybe a boat trip, leave them to the sea."

A light broke into the room as a figure came through the same small hatch that Johnston had. Holding her hands up, Hope tried to watch what was happening but the light was once again blinding.

"That's Macleod!" shouted Johnston.

Brace made a sudden move towards the figure as it stood up and Hope instantly reacted by running forward and throwing her shoulder into Johnston. Due to the lack of light, there was no way to judge her tackle and she instead turned as she threw herself forward, driving her shoulder at where she thought Brace was. Her shoulder struck his rump and her legs clattered into his, bringing him down.

Macleod had just stood up and had heard the footsteps charging on the wooden floor. He was not as spritely as Hope but he did have a quick mind and simply stepped sideways several times until he hit a piece of furniture. To his side, he heard the commotion as Hope now scrapped on the floor with Brace. He was at a loss to help and desperately felt along the wall for a light switch. There was none. But then he found what may have been a bureau and a lamp on it. Macleod fiddled with the connections until he found a switch and light suddenly bathed the room.

208

Hope was on the floor, turned on her front and Brace was positioned on top and behind her, holding her hair, looking like he was about to drive her face into the wooden floor. Johnston was across the room, eyes struggling in the sudden brilliance. Macleod ran straight over to Brace as he went to plant Hope's face forward, and kicked the man's gut with all that he had.

Brace had not seen it coming and he curled at the blow but was still on top of Hope. Macleod kicked again before Brace could react and then dove at him knocking him off Hope but became entangled himself. As he tried to get to his feet, a hand grabbed his shoulder pinning him and he was struck hard with an elbow.

Macleod had not been on the streets of Glasgow in his earlier days as a policeman without learning a few tricks of the trade and he managed to reach back and jab a finger into Brace's eye. The man recoiled off him and Macleod rolled away, grabbing the corner of a chair and managing to stand. But Brace was back on his feet and coming for Macleod. As Brace stretched out his hands for the Inspector, Macleod noticed that the light in the room was moving, as if shaken about. Then there came a loud crack and a shattering of glass as Hope drove the lamp into Brace's head.

There was solid thud as Brace hit the floor followed by a tinkling of glass and ceramic pieces following him down. Everything went dark again and Macleod could see nothing. But he knew where Brace had fallen and jumped on top of him. Searching with his hands he found the man's face but he was unresponsive. Taking off his belt in the dark, Macleod began to tie Brace's hands up behind his back.

"Can you see Johnston?" asked Macleod.

"See? How can I see? I just broke the lamp," said Hope.

"I have Brace, just finishing off his bonds. Get Johnston."

"Yes, sir," said Hope.

"Mr Johnston, it's all over, we have your thug." Hope was trying to sound professional but she was breathing deeply after her struggles with Brace and the adrenalin was pumping through her veins.

"I think not," said Johnston, his voice stretched. "I know this place, I helped Macaulay design the whole house and I set the deadlier parts. The easily removed safeties were my doing. That thug Brace couldn't do such neat handiwork. It was a pity about Macaulay because he was such a talent, such an imaginative mind. But he panicked when they upped the ante. Wouldn't join us. And despite being a thug, Brace is right. I only walk away when you all die. So be prepared for it, both of you, for you won't leave this room."

Hope was making her way steadily in the dark toward the voice. She could just about judge where Johnston was and in her bare feet she managed to mask her footsteps well on the wooden floor. He wouldn't know she was coming. He was nearly in reach.

Macleod was barely listening to Johnston as he removed Brace's belt and tied up the man's feet. But something in Johnston's tone made him start to take notice. The room, the man had said, will not leave the room. He had no weapons. He was physically no match for Hope, probably not even for Macleod on a level playing field. *I know this place.* He said, *I know this place.*

"Hope! Get down! Get away from his voice!"

"But, sir?"

"Now!"

Macleod heard the mechanism in the dark. A whir of possibly cogs and pulleys and then the forceful swoosh of something being propelled before it slammed into the wall. Macleod waited for movement, waited to hear Hope's voice. But there was nothing.

"McGrath? Hope?"

There was a murmur in the dark that moved away from Macleod. It was accompanied by shuffling and Macleod's heart rose. But he could also hear footsteps in the dark that were not Hope's. Johnston was after her and Macleod could not just sit and wait in the void, leaving Hope to her own devices. Listening to the sounds carefully, Macleod turned himself until he was pointing at the feet moving on the floor. Surely, he had it right. There was nothing for it but to run in the dark and pray he hit the right person.

Taking off at a clip, Macleod lowered his shoulder as he ran, twisting further as he reached what he thought was his target. He sailed through the air as he lifted from his feet and anticipated colliding with someone. But nothing came and he hit the polished floor and slid into a wall. He groaned as the pain seized his shoulder and he rolled in agony. As he turned over in pain, his feet caught something and he heard a cry, then someone stumbling, before Johnston yelled.

"No! Dear God, no!"

There was the sound of heavy breathing and the room suddenly lit up. Macleod tried, and failed, to raise a hand to cover his eyes and was blinded almost immediately. There was a wind blowing, something that did not surprise Macleod anymore, but Johnston's reaction was cutting into him. Once he had tried to protect a man from drug dealers on an estate as they came towards him. They were hooded and carried

211

firearms and the man beside Macleod knew he was a dead man. They would leave Macleod while the masks were on but not their intended victim. That man's cry matched what he was hearing from Johnston.

"Can you see him, Hope?"

"I can't move, sir, the last trap caught me. I've dragged it but it's got my top and I can't move anywhere quick."

His shoulder ringing in pain Macleod reached forward, swinging his hand blindly, to and fro. He used his feet to push himself along the ground towards Johnston's screaming voice but there was nothing. And then he touched fingers with someone. Again he stretched and Macleod managed to grasp a hand.

"I have you, Johnston, hold on. I have you."

There came a loud roar like some ancient deity of old and then some words spoken in a language Macleod had never heard. But Johnston knew what it meant for he screamed. And then the hand was whipped away from Macleod. There was the sound of bone being crushed and flesh rendered. Macleod was glad he could not see as Johnston's screams fell silent.

And then the lights in the room came on. In one corner was Brace, barely conscious and tied up by the hands and feet with belts. Hope sat on the floor, a curved hook caught on her blouse top which was a deep pink. Macleod prayed she had no serious injuries with that amount of blood on her.

Macleod was lying a small distance from a wall with his hand outstretched to the opposite wall which now had a hole in it. There were sets of teeth and a figure of some creature around them. And the remains of Johnston among those teeth. Macleod looked away quickly.

"Is that it, sir?" asked Hope.

"No, McGrath. We're knee deep in snow outside, a criminal, confined by the flimsiest of fixings and some seriously injured people downstairs. No, the day's not complete. But we won the game." Macleod sighed and then looked up at Hope. He nodded at her blouse. "But you took a battering."

"Pig's blood, sir."

Macleod shook his head and laughed. It was inappropriate and he didn't know why he was doing it but he laughed anyway.

Chapter 25

Macleod was standing in a large luminescent jacket with the word Police on the back in blue, looking at the house that had been his torment over the previous days. The weather had broken and the sky was clear giving the house a stunning aspect with all the snow gathered about. It was cold and the coffee he held in his hands was more of a heat source to him than refreshment.

"You did well, Macleod. You both did. Hell of a mess though; the papers will have a field day with this."

"Yes Ma'am. Some big names in the house." His boss had arrived on the scene soon after the initial emergency services had got there. Hope's signal from the small boat had been enough but the weather had been too wild for anyone to make a rescue attempt. Once the weather had started to die down, they had come and Macleod had waved down the helicopter that had flown over. The single-track road out to the house was now being cleared and the ferry runs of different helicopters would soon cease.

"I find it hard they would have wanted to kill me, Macleod. Some of the celebrities, yes, but why me? I'm not exactly that well known." His boss shivered a little but Macleod believed the cold was not to blame.

"But you are a figure Ma'am. The diversity agenda we're following—you've been very prominent. I think it was that. You made some speeches about people their group don't want in society. Appears that was enough."

"And is McGrath all right? I haven't seen her yet."

"No, she's not. Running around, trying to do things when she should really be getting seen to. I don't think we'll shake this one that easily," said Macleod.

"Should have been me, Macleod."

"Yes Ma'am, it should have. But I doubt your husband would agree."

His boss looked at him and her eyes softened to a pity. "No, he would not."

The pair stood looking at the house until a junior officer ran up to the Chief Inspector and passed her a message Macleod did not hear. He was close enough; he just was beyond caring. Someone else could do the wrap up this time. All he wanted was to get on a flight back to Glasgow and to see Jane. He wanted things other than this.

It was less than an hour ago when they had taken Mrs Johnston off to a helicopter and she had walked right past him. The woman was a mess, sobbing and laden with the guilt that her husband had orchestrated all this. And yet she tried to reach out to Macleod, tried to say thank you for saving her life, and the others. But Macleod could still hear that scream after Jermaine Johnston had tripped over his legs. He could not look at the woman.

Macleod heard his boss say something. Then she said it again. He turned to her and stared blankly. "Sorry, I was somewhere else."

"Okay. I was saying that with the links they have left here

215

we should be able to trace this group, get some ideas about them. We know there is a group like this but we have been struggling to get any hold. But then again it was not a high priority as they had not carried out any acts and we thought it was a rich-boys club, one that might fire out propaganda and that. There was no indication of this." It was almost said as an apology but Macleod did not need one.

"They'll be looking for someone with first-hand experience of the group to come on board . . ."

"No!" said Macleod, a little too firmly.

"I wasn't asking you, Seoras. I need you right here where you are. But McGrath, it would be a good opportunity for her, advance her career."

"Yes, it would," was Macleod's resigned comment.

As he made the comment, he saw Hope emerging from the front door, talking to one of the Scenes of Crime personnel. She was animated, and to some she would have been her usual industrious self. But there was a lack of lustre in her that Macleod could see. He thought of her going home to an empty house, and then all this would come after her. He had that happen several times before he met Jane, before Hope had started working with him, and he would wish it on no one.

"Did you garner much else before we all arrived?" asked his boss.

"Not a lot. I had a son who had lost his mother, a wife who had lost her husband, a teenager whose boyfriend had been trying to kill her, a daughter who had lost her dad and a man who was grieving his partner. McGrath and I were the only two who had not lost someone in there. Macaulay had wanted to provide a horror weekend, a time to be loose amongst madness. You had to see the things he built, carefully crafted monstrosities dripped in pig's blood and all other sorts of effects. But he failed to see the horror of what he was part of until it was too late."

"So it was only Brace and Johnston who carried this out?"

"Once constructed, Macaulay was an innocent. He died once they tried to bring him fully on board and he refused—at least that's my take. But the housekeeper, Mrs Smith, she was in on it too. Much to her son's horror."

Once again, there was silence between them and Macleod knew that feeling of wanting to scream and shout at all of this death and madness but was instead maintaining that policeman's poise, holding things in for a better time to release them.

Hope had now made her way towards them and came before her bosses, putting on that poise Macleod was such an expert in.

"I think I've passed on everything, ma'am, sir. Just going to take five minutes over there if that's all right."

The Chief Inspector nodded and as Hope started walking, Macleod made his apologies to his boss and followed her. She did not look back but kept walking until she reached the beach and stood at the change from snow to sand. Macleod joined her looking out into the small sea loch. Normally the area would get a dusting of snow and there would be bits of heather and bog land darkening the colour, but after this storm, the land seemed to have been completely purified.

"Not sure I have ever seen Glasgow like this, totally white. There's hardly a drop of anything else. It's so pristine," said Hope.

"That's the beauty of up here, the weather can be rough but then you get these moments when you see the real package. A little bit of sun always helps though." Macleod looked at Hope and he saw a faint smile.

"Wasn't sure I'd get to see it. But you just go on, do the job. Or else you wouldn't make it." Hope was quiet for a moment and then suddenly spoke. "Johnston, that scream . . ."

"Yes," said Macleod, "that scream. If they offer help, take it. If they don't, find it. It's not my first and they don't go."

The pair stood as the sea rolled in gently before backing away. There was a line of seaweed that had been throw up onto the beach and which was mixed in with the snow. It was not a sight Macleod had often seen. He looked at the loch and then turned letting his eyes roam across the landscape but carefully avoiding the house.

"I might leave Glasgow, if Jane will come."

"Leave," queried Hope. "Just Glasgow, or do you mean the force too?"

"Just Glasgow. Maybe Inverness, maybe over here. I don't know. Just feel I want to go home, back to islands. Or at least the highlands if I can't make that work. It's different up here. Can you see that?"

"Yes, it's quite something."

Macleod watched her standing, looking out to sea, her red hair blowing in the wind and found himself pitying her returning to no one at home. She'd need help with this one.

"Sunday lunch."

"Sorry? What do you mean, Seoras?" asked Hope.

"Come around Sunday; Jane's a decent cook. You'll have plans to discuss. Career plans."

"What career plans? It was you that said you wanted to move."

"Trust me," said Macleod. "Lunch on Sunday. Career plans.

And a bit of company for when you hear the scream."

Hope nodded and then gave Macleod a gentle smile before turning to look out at the sea again. Macleod joined her and watched the waves rise and fall in their steady motion. They said the sea soothed and it did. Every tiny crash as the small breakers made it to shore, every sudden sucking drain as the sea retreated from between rocks. With his back to the house, and a mind that was metaphorically walking away from it, he thought about how to convince Jane to come to the islands.

About the Author

GR Jordan is a self-published author who finally decided at forty that in order to have an enjoyable lifestyle, his creative beast within would have to be unleashed. His books mirror that conflict in life where acts of decency contend with self-promotion, goodness stares in horror at evil, and kindness blindsides us when we at our worst. Corrupting our world with his parade of wondrous and horrific characters, he highlights everyday tensions with fresh eyes whilst taking his methodical, intelligent mainstays on a roller-coaster ride of dilemmas, all the while suffering the banter of their provocative sidekicks.

A graduate of Loughborough University where he masqueraded as a chemical engineer but ultimately played American football, Gary had worked at changing the shape of cereal flakes and pulled a pallet truck for a living. Watching vegetables freeze at -40'C was another career highlight and he was also one of the Scottish Highlands "blind" air traffic controllers.

These days he has graduated to answering a telephone to people in trouble before telephoning other people to sort it out.

Having flirted with most places in the UK, he is now based in the Isle of Lewis in Scotland where his free time is spent between raising a young family with his wife, writing, figuring out how to work a loom and caring for a small flock of chickens. Luckily, his writing is influenced by his varied work and life experience as the chickens have not been the poetical inspiration he had hoped for!

You can connect with me on:
- https://grjordan.com
- https://twitter.com/carpetless
- ttps://facebook.com/carpetlessleprechaun

Subscribe to my newsletter:
- https://mailchi.mp/bf149bd0218b/crescendo

Also by G R Jordan

G R Jordan writes across multiple genres including dark and action adventure fantasy, feel good fantasy, mystery thriller and horror fantasy. Below are a selection of his work grouped together in their genres, starting with the popular Austerley & Kirkgordon action adventure fantasy. Whilst all books are available across online stores, signed copies are available at his personal shop.

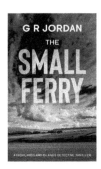

The Small Ferry: A Highlands and Islands Detective Thriller (Highlands & Islands Detective Book 4)

A dreich day for a crossing and a small ferry packed to the gills. After off-loading one man sits dead at the wheel of the last remaining car. Can Macleod find the connections between the passengers, before the killer strikes again?

Macleod and McGrath return to Cromarty when a man is found dead at the wheel of his car on the local ferry. As the passengers are identified, the trail extends across the highlands and islands as past deeds are paid back in full. Can the seasoned pair hunt down a killer before their butchery spreads across the land?

"The Small Ferry" is the fourth Highlands and Islands Detective thriller and brings the odd pair back to the Black Isle when the quiet routine of the Firth is broken apart by a strange death. If you like murder mysteries set amongst the beautiful north of Scotland and its wild coastline and islands, then you'll love the adventures of Macleod and McGrath.

When there's so much going on, it can be hard to see what's happening!

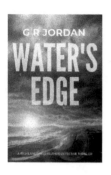

Water's Edge: A Highlands and Islands Detective Thriller (Highlands & Islands Detective Book 1)
A body discovered by the rocks. A broken detective returns to a scene of past tragedy. Will the pain of the past prevent him from seeing the present?

Detective Inspector Macleod returns to his island home twenty years after the painful loss of his wife. With a disposition forged in strong religious conservatism, he must bond with his new partner, the free spirited and upcoming female star of the force, to seek the killer of a young woman and shine a light on the evil beneath the surface. To do so, he must once again stand in the place where he lost everything. Only at the water's edge, will everything be made new.

The rising tide brings all things to the surface.

The Bothy: A Highlands and Islands Detective Thriller (Highlands & Islands Detective Book 2)
Two bodies in a burnt out love nest. A cultish lifestyle and children moulded by domination. Can Macleod unravel the Black Isle mystery before the killer dispenses judgement again?

DI Macleod heads for the Black Isle as winter sets in to unravel the mystery of two lovers in a burned out bothy. With his feisty partner DC McGrath, he must unravel the connection between a family living under a cultish cloud and a radio station whose staff are being permanently retired. In the dark of winter, can Macleod shine a light on the shadowy relationships driving a killer to their murderous tasks?

Forgetting your boundaries has never been so deadly!

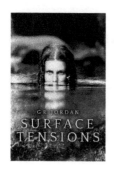

Surface Tensions (Island Adventures Book 1)
Mermaids sighted near a Scottish island. A town exploding in anger and distrust. And Donald's got to get the sexiest fish in town, back in the water.

"Surface Tensions" is the first story in a series of Island adventures from the pen of G R Jordan. If you love comic moments, cosy adventures and light fantasy action, then you'll love these tales with a twist.Get the book that amazon readers said, "perfectly captures life in the Scottish Hebrides" and that explores "human nature at its best and worst".

Something's stirring the water!

Austerley & Kirgordon Adventures Box Set: Books 1-3 and Origin stories 1-3 (Austerley& Kirkgordon)
A retired bodyguard looking for a little fun before it's too late. An obsessive Professor, seeking the darkest things of life. And an Elder god seeking to rule the world, if they can't stop him.

Join Austerley and Kirkgordon on the rollercoaster ride that is their first three adventures. Comprising 3 full novels as well as 3 accompanying origin novellettes, this collection will introduce you to a polarised duo that are the world's best hope. Joining them for the adventure are a myriad of strange characters, bizarre anmals, evil humans and the UK's finest agents from its most secret department.

As one reviewer put it, "If you like Lovecraft, Poe, or Conan Doyle you will like this book. If you like tv show like Buffy the Vampire Slayer, Supernatural, Being Human, or X-Files you will like this book."

So take a chance on a molotov cocktail of a duo and see how to save the world on the wild side.